The Teacher's Heart

Michel Prince

The Growing Strong Series
Book 4

Published by
Satin Romance
An Imprint of Melange Books, LLC
White Bear Lake, MN 55110
www.satinromance.com

ISBN: 978-1-68046-424-5

Cover Design by Ashley Byland from Redbird Designs

Author Note:

Three years ago, I sat down to write a novella about a hot father, but he fell in love with a woman who had three amazing friends. Their story was too great to hold in a few pages, instead a full novel was born. The friends demanded their own stories. I went back and forth unsure if I could write a f/f story because one of the women had no interest in men and I wasn't leaving her behind. No one gets left behind once they're part of the Growing Strong Mafia.

Over the past three years Gabbie, Mary Beth, Sarah and Mandy have made me laugh, cry and brought my writing to a new level. I'll miss them more than any characters I've written before. Whether it was learning Spanish, figuring out the pronouns in a same sex relationship or getting the one who'd sworn off love all together I will miss the girls and a friendship that should be used as an example in the dictionary.

Chapter One

*"Man may have discovered fire,
but women discovered how to play with it."*
—Candace Bushnell, Sex and the City

With a quick knock on the condo door, Mandy Butler leaned on the doorjamb and waited. Pretending to be bored, she examined her fingernails until the door opened to reveal Ashton Gilmore in all his hunk-tastic glory. His toothbrush dangled from between his full lips and his blond Abercrombie-type hair had the windblown falseness only a fool still fell for. Mandy smiled at the pair of soft, black pajama pants that hung a little low on his waist, sharing the luscious V that pointed to her favorite part of him.

"Your girlfriend just asked my roommate to marry her on local cable access."

"I was there," he replied with a mouthful of foaming toothpaste obscuring the words.

He opened the door wider to usher her in as he went to the kitchen and completed the whole rinse and spit from his toothbrush.

"You know what this means don't you?" Mandy asked as she eyed his backside like a fat kid eyes cake. He leaned over the sink to catch the water in his mouth, giving her a better view.

"You'll have to find other ways to sneak and fuck me." Ashton snatched a towel and wiped his lips before turning around.

"Oh please, that's so never happening again. You were there, I was there…but tonight they come home like I don't live in my own apartment."

1

"Uh huh." He smirked. No doubt he knew all too well why she knocked on his door, and not Gabbie Thomas', her best friend, who happened to have an extra bedroom.

Her thumb was the problem. It wouldn't keep itself under control. Absently it swiped the corner of his mouth where a bit of toothpaste lingered. He caught her wrist in his hand and spun her around until she was pinned against the sink.

"Amanda Butler, why are you here?"

"Your girlfriend of like a decade just dumped you on local cable access for another woman," she said mournfully as she held in her gasp from the hardness pressing against her hip. "Most men would be crushed. Are you crushed? You know, questioning your manhood and all?"

"Should I be?" he asked while taking a long lingering stroke from her hip to her stomach. Standing a good six-two to her five-seven had made leaning down a necessary evil at times. His lips brushed against her neck and she used her free hand to brace herself on the counter. "Do you doubt my abilities as a man?"

Somewhere deep down inside, she wanted to scream no. No to infinity. No because she actually missed his body in the morning, but she couldn't.

She couldn't tell the man who'd flipped her life upside down for the past two and a half months that the only reason she came home was to find him. The sneaking around on his closeted girlfriend of ten years sent her in a tizzy. She hated the arrangement, but then again, she'd been conceived from a somewhat similar "arrangement" made between her mother and father. One where she would sit back and be a single mother and he would go on raising his other family without so much as a word to Mandy about who he really was.

It had been Ash's loyalty to Karen, his best friend, that kindled her attraction to him. She wasn't one to have a guy, or girl, around for more than a day or two. Not believing in the whole monogamy thing had her at odds with her best friends, though they'd still do anything for her. Gabbie, Mary Beth, and her current roomy, Sarah, were the type of ride-or-die bitches a girl could go her whole life without meeting.

"Amanda…" he growled, and chills ran up her spine. Men didn't call her Amanda—they preferred the cute and flirty Mandy. She preferred being the cute and flirty Mandy. But now…now she wanted to be Amanda. The Amanda who would spend the night and find Ashton Gilmore lying next to her in the morning. "Should I be questioning my manhood?"

"No," she gasped as her gut clenched. Fingers curled, bunching her shirt as he removed it and tasted her stomach.

He had dropped to his knees in front of her and took time to savor her, not just pull down her pants and take her hard and fast the way she wanted him to. The way he usually did. No, this time they had something she'd been avoiding…true alone time.

"Wait," she panicked, but her words went unheard. Or if they were heard they were completely ignored.

Either way, Ashton turned her around and removed her panties. She could have easily kept her feet firmly planted. That's what people who said wait would have done. Instead she lifted first her right foot, then left, to which she got a sweet nip on her butt. He did know how to get her ass going…or not going as the case may be.

~ * ~

The last thing Ashton Gilmore expected to see at his door last night was Mandy. Sure, they'd been sleeping together for the past few months, but she had made it more than clear it was more out of boredom than actual attraction. He thought he knew better. She was a mystery to him.

If he thought last night was a surprise, this morning was downright monumental. Curled into his arms, with her head resting on his chest, lay the dark-haired beauty. Deep mahogany hair verging on black cascaded across a pillow, and he missed her hazel eyes with their brown speckles. Learning the origin of the eyes made the secrets and lies he'd been living with seem like child's play.

Tapping the volume button on the remote, he tried to focus on the commentator. He had been reading the subtitles, but the sun crept across his room and highlighted Mandy's hips, and then her chest. By the time the rays reflected off the smooth skin of her neck, he'd been entranced. Sadly, a flash on the screen of Karen made him refocus and reengage.

Mandy stirred, but stayed asleep. Even in her slumber her fingertips were so gentle and delicate as they unconsciously traced his body. It took everything in him to not squirm from the sensation—and he had lift off. Not a bad thing considering what had taken place the night before. Hell, the only bad thing about last night was that it had been so good, he worried he may have peaked. Maybe it was all downhill from here. Mandy's leg wrapped around his hip and she woke suddenly.

"Oh shit," she said as she quickly uncurled, leaving him cold and searching. "Fuck. Fuck. Triple fuck…what time is it?"

"Seven…" he craned his neck to see the digital display on his clock. "Sixteen."

"Mother trucker." Her quick switch into appropriate swear words always made him smile.

"What's the matter?"

"I have work," she balked. "I'm a teacher. Getting there before the kids is advised."

"Jesus, I just realized I fucked a kindergarten teacher. Totally forgot to scratch that off my list."

"Funny, jack hole." She scrambled into the kitchen, and he swung his legs around to follow her. The closest thing to the bed were a pair of sweatpants, which he threw on and then followed her. "You're a damn genius. Plus, I'm not a kindergarten teacher."

Stomping her shoe on, she bent back to pull out the back of it. Her fingers tangled through her hair and she rushed to his bathroom.

"Magilla, how do you not have a brush?" she spat. "Seriously I don't buy that windblown shit."

Ashton used his index finger to open the top drawer. Mandy glared at him as she retrieved the brush and violently pulled it through her hair.

"Time?" she snapped. He leaned back to look in his bedroom.

"Seven nineteen."

"Shit. Shit. Triple shit."

"How late are you?" he asked as he scratched his belly.

"Are you kidding me?" she pointed the brush at his crotch. "You seriously think I have time to fuck you?"

He hadn't thought about that, having dropped to half-mast after the scramble and blur that was Mandy's usual morning routine. He just wanted to know why she was in a panic. Everyone was late once in a while, and wasn't she part owner of the school anyway? A fancy private one no less.

"I had an itch."

"And I'm the only one who can scratch it…yeah, yeah. I've heard it all before."

"That's a horrible line. I have much better ones."

Mandy scoffed. "I forgot you're a master."

"I'm not a twelve-year-old boy."

"I tend to stay away from felonies." She pushed past him and toward the counter to grab her keys. "I assume you don't."

"Boys aren't really my style."

"I meant twelve-year-olds."

Ashton sighed and leaned on his counter. He knew he'd be going through this routine again someday, even though Mandy had sworn this would be the last time. Just like last time and the time before that.

"Do I get a kiss goodbye?" he yawned.

"Don't let me keep you awake. Don't you have a job to do?"

"Yes."

"Then why are you sitting here?"

"I'm getting ready. I've been working for the past three hours."

Mandy stood in the doorway shifting from one side to the other before taking off and leaving Ashton confused as usual. Returning to his room, he pulled out a suit and continued watching the talking heads. Conservatives didn't know what to do. Karen Schroeder was their best bet to win the congressional seat in the fifth district, but coming out had thrown the religious right into a tailspin.

"And what about Ashton Gilmore?" the female co-host said as she flashed a picture of Karen and Ashton snuggling at a picnic. *"What is his part in the whole charade? Did he play along with the deception, or was he as big of a fool as the rest of the state of Minnesota?"*

He flipped off the TV. That was unfair. Karen only had a small area of which she was the state representative. It wasn't like the *whole* state had been duped. Really the only ones who cared were Karen's parents. Last night Ash's dad had laughed with him on the way home on the phone. Carlton Gilmore came from money and didn't take too much seriously. After his mother left his dad, Ash let slip about Karen, so he already knew.

The talking heads had been calling him everything from a stooge to a fool. In their mind, he'd just lost the love of his life. Still, Karen was a good friend, but his lifestyle was definitely about to change.

After showering and getting dressed, he went in search of his wayward girlfriend.

"Morning," Sarah said as she opened the door with just-been-fucked blonde hair. At least Karen had fun. "She's still asleep."

"She does know she has people wanting her to govern, right?"

"Know…versus care…" Sarah sighed with a slight yawn.

"How you doing?"

"Fine, still can't believe it."

"Me either. Guess I said the magic words to her."

"What was that?" Sarah asked as she trudged to the couch and flopped as her eyes drooped.

"You were done."

"Guess I wasn't."

"No guessing at all." Ashton made his way to Karen and woke her with a cup of coffee and the news that she couldn't go back.

"Morning, sunshine. You look worse than me. Did someone stay up past her bedtime?"

"Usually when I have to deal with your bullshit I've had two cups." Karen swirled her coffee a bit before swallowing her go-go juice. "Now, what do I need to know?"

Ashton updated her on the cable and local news coverage as well as the information Howard had told him. Sponsorships, wins and losses, the interview requests, and where she stood in the polls.

"Because I'm from the LGBT community?" she spat at the request from *Lavender* wanting an interview.

He laughed as he passed her a croissant. She wasn't part of the LGBT community, she'd been locked in the closet too damn long to even understand it. Although Karen's phone had been turned off for most of the night, she had checked in with her family…at least the ones who would talk to her. That had brought her some solace.

"Maybe I didn't lose my whole family then," she said as she took the top off her coffee and swirled again.

"I doubt it. And you know your mom will come back if you win the primary."

"And if I don't?"

"Give her an extra week. You know she can't go a whole week without calling you about something."

"I hope so." Karen finished her coffee and shook out the night. "Any chance you have a change of clothes with you?"

"I'm nothing if not your humble servant."

"Thank you, I know you're probably getting some backlash."

"Nothing I can't handle. I've been around your rages. The shit I'm getting is child's play."

"Ash," Karen said apologetically as she dug through the toiletry bag he'd brought with him for a brush. "I need to know you're okay."

"I'm tougher than you think, my love."

"No going back from this one," she sighed. "I can't really claim I was on allergy medicine or something."

"Nope," Ash replied as he kissed the crown of her head and then looked at a picture on Sarah's nightstand of the Growing Strong Mafia, the nickname earned by Mandy, Sarah, Gabbie, and Mary Beth. The four women had their arms around each other, laughing after a softball game. "Even if you could, would you really want to hurt her?"

Karen looked at the picture and shook her head.

Thirty minutes later, they were in his car with Karen back in power suit mode. In a black DKNY skirt, silk camisole, and two button jacket with an American flag pin on the lapel, she was ready for primetime. Luckily, she had a handful of clothes at his house for emergencies. Her hair…well, the auburn tresses had been brushed out and quaffed in her helmet style.

"Do I still have a job?" he asked as they pulled into her parking space at her congressional office.

"Why wouldn't you?"

"My main job was being your beard. I was man candy that kept the girls jealous at what an awesome catch I was."

"You're also an advisor. Here to help me, you know, make decisions."

"How are we playing this? Am I your fool or cover?"

"I'm tired of lying," Karen sighed with a voice full of hope instead of fear. It made him smile. After all these years, she had finally found peace. "You've always been my best friend."

"Got you."

When they opened the car door, they could hear the reporters on the steps outside the parking garage. He was sure that was the closest Tyron the security guard would let them. And even then, they would be getting the patented stare of not interested, don't care, and get the fuck away from my job.

"You ready, sweetie?" he asked as he took her cool hand. "You seem petrified."

"No comment, getting back to the campaign trail, and governing for my constituents."

"I'm still voting for you."

"Are you even registered?" she teased.

"I'm hurt." He nudged her as they walked. "You know Howard gave me a bomb pop for registering a few years ago."

They were laughing as blasts of light blinded them from three different cameras. His hand instantly shot up so when his vision returned he'd be able to see through. His other hand he tightly wrapped around Karen's slender waist. She curled against his side and they made their way through without saying a word. Not now, but later maybe, when Howard filled them in on everything.

Settling into the desk in his office, he let Karen decompress while he checked emails and finally turned his phone on. Only seventeen messages. Not bad for ignoring it for six hours. Right as he was about to check the voicemails, his phone rang with a two, zero, two number.

"Ashton Gilmore," he answered, unsure of who from Washington D.C. would be calling him.

"Hello, Mr. Gilmore, this is Victor Turner, I'm the current liaison for the Midwest district of the Republican National Committee. How are you this morning?"

"Fine, and yourself?" Victor didn't need an introduction. He'd more than made himself a fixture last spring when he talked Karen into running for the open House seat. She was part of his big plan to flip eight districts in the Midwest alone.

"I've been trying to reach your candidate."

"I'm sorry. I can put you through to her right now if you need."

"Not just yet. I did call to speak to you."

"Then speak," Ashton replied while picking up a pen and doodling on the Month at a Glance calendar on his desk. There were still a few eights that needed their circles colored in.

"I understand this may be a hard time for you and you're trying to figure out where you went wrong."

"Not really."

"So you knew?"

"Mr. Turner, if you'd like to talk to Representative Schroeder—"

"Ash, let me tell you what we here at the RNC think of you." Ashton's stomach tightened as he moved on to the nines. "Your sacrifice for your beliefs are tremendous. It is obvious to not only me, but those at the top of the RNC you knew about Representative Schroeder long before the rest of us, but you saw how she could benefit the party and sacrificed years of your life to be by her side."

"It wasn't a sacrifice." Ashton's jaw clenched. "Representative Schroeder has an integrity that can't be matched."

"There we disagree, Ash," Victor said. "I see someone with a bit more, and we want him to come out to Washington as a part of our strategy team."

Ash dropped the pen from his hand as he sat back. "You want me to be a member of the national committee?"

"We've looked at old videos of you and her. This game you two played has had you thinking on your feet quite a bit."

It had become second nature to him—the evasion and instant body checks. Was he close enough? Was she? Public displays of affection and all the rest.

"You're being called up into the big leagues, Ashton. It's just a trial run with a few candidates and issues that would need your ideas and input. Then we'd see about making it permanent."

"I'm part of the Schroeder campaign right now." Ashton wasn't sure what he wanted to do. He wasn't even sure he was ready to be a grown-up.

"Stay on it, hell, she might even make it past the primaries. Right

now, we'd just need a few days from you in Washington here and there."
Victor paused. "Let's keep this between you and I for right now."

"And how will I explain running off in the middle of the campaign to Representative Schroeder?"

"Tell her she's not the only one who found a lover."

"Funny."

"She's fucking with our core, but bringing in new supporters." Ash heard him take a beat before words spewed that couldn't be taken back. "The leadership is still trying to figure out, what if anything, to do with her."

"When we win the primary will the RNC help with funding?"

"Of course. We back all our party elected candidates."

For his entire adult life Ashton had looked out for Karen. He didn't even think he knew how to do anything else. He'd never had another job, but as she moved on with her life, it was starting to seem like she didn't need him to be a crutch anymore. Now Ash would need one to become a grown-up and decide what he wanted out of life, instead of helping Karen get what she wanted.

"You wanna help? Then you really help. Commit. She's in a district you're trying to flip."

"A lot of candidates are," Victor deadpanned back.

Wendy poked her head over his cubical wall. "Hey, Ash, the Snelling women are here."

"I'll be right in there." He turned back into his cell phone. "When's the first meeting?"

"After the primaries have finalized so we can see where the funds need to go and work through any problems."

He stared down at the calendar. Circled dates with important notes stared up at him. His job, his duties, his life.

"Send me a ticket, I'll make it work."

~ * ~

Mandy dug through the back of her car and found what she needed—a black polo with the Growing Strong Montessori logo embroidered on it. Thank God. It was a bit wrinkled, but that she could knock out quickly before the students arrived. Her fear was having to get home and then back to the school in time. This way she'd be on time, maybe even a little early. With her polo over her arm she walked in and waved at Mary Beth greeting kids at the front door today. She cut left and headed to see if Gabbie was in her office.

Mandy had the good fortune to meet Gabbie at age seven. The day that lives in infamy among those in the Oakdale, Minnesota area. Four girls walked into tee-ball practice. Only two knew each other, Mary Beth and Sarah, but by the end of practice, plans had been finalized without even so much as a word to their parents. Almost twenty years had passed.

Through the glass and wooden door of the principal's office she saw Gabbie's belly. Her now four-month pregnant belly. On her five-two frame, the baby had nowhere to go, but out, and Gabbie was taking it in stride that she'd be a beached whale in less than two months.

"Hey," Mandy called as she poked her head in the door right as Gabbie sat down. Her midnight onyx hair was pulled up into a ponytail with two sparkly barrettes on either side, holding back loose strands. Mandy assumed the addition was Gabbie's newly adopted three-year-old daughter, Claire's, idea. "I crashed at your house last night."

"All right," Gabbie replied without going any further, and then looked at the clock on her desk. "Is this a more than once thing, or was it just last night when you really needed your toenails painted?"

"Karen came to our place last night, I just didn't think the newly engaged wanted a third wheel." Mandy leaned against the doorjamb. "Then again, I should have asked. You know the whole three is better than two thing."

"No…no, I don't."

"Says the woman about to bring a third child into her home."

Gabbie clicked her pen a few times. "The first two were there when I arrived. I didn't bring them."

"Where are my two favorite Children's Housers?"

"In the care center."

"Do you have matching barrettes today?"

Gabbie absently felt the side of her head and smiled.

"Yes, never wore them as a kid, but suddenly I need to be a girl."

"It was bound to happen. When I catch Maury in makeup, I'll have determined Claire rules the world."

"He's got Charlie to protect him."

"All right, gotta knock out some wrinkles and I'll be all good to go."

Growing Strong Montessori started as a daycare center with a very different name, Betty's Bundles of Love. Buying the established daycare center let the four eighteen-year-olds have an income already established and Betty loved stepping back slowly so the girls could learn the ropes. Gabbie, the over analyzer, researched all sorts of child care and learning methods to discover the Montessori method. The rest of the girls went along for the ride. All in an effort to help Mary Beth, who foolishly got knocked up senior year. None of them had direction, aside from playing softball on partial scholarships, so helping out Mary Beth seemed as good as any other plan in the world.

"Ms. Mand," Charlie, Gabbie's other adopted child, sang as he came in the room and held tightly to her legs. His cocoa skin and mahogany eyes mirrored his much older brother Case, Gabbie's husband. "Can you eat lunch at my's table?"

"You are the first to ask, so yes, sir." Mandy smiled and stroked his tight fade a bit.

Soon after, Claire, his twin sister, bounded in the classroom with her hair in two afro-puffs and tiny barrettes. Normally they wouldn't have siblings in the same classroom, but this was the first year of them being a licensed school and they only had one class per level.

As her day started, she smiled at her students and made sure they were all set to learn. Calm was the word for her classroom. With twenty-three children between the ages of three and six, one wouldn't think it was possible, but even with eyes eager to play and learn, the children headed off to their tasks. Most of their students had transitioned from their daycare center and knew how to behave. The Montessori learning environment was unlike any other she'd seen. Growing up she'd sat next to boys eating paste instead of gluing one piece of construction paper to another. In her classroom, the kids mastered skills like tying shoes, cooking, and cleaning, all while discovering math and reading skills she hadn't mastered until the third grade. Well, honestly fourth.

"Ms. Mand," a curly haired blonde named Chloe called as she skipped into the room. "I need a lesson."

"You do, huh?" Mandy smiled at the bright blue eyes of the four-year-old.

"Yep, I wanna know how to do the pieces."

"The pieces?" she asked, looking around her room.

Chloe walked to the science shelf where a bowl and ten objects were on a tray.

"Okay, I'll give a lesson on that so you'll know what to do, but let's see if we can get a few more classmates interested too."

Chloe went in search of friends, and Jasmine, Mandy's assistant teacher, came in with a handful of groceries along with Drew's mother. With spiral curls coming to her shoulders, Jasmine's smile always seemed framed by joy. She obviously loved and took advantage of the freedom of the Montessori method and thinking. The last thing the Growing Strong Mafia were going to tell her was she couldn't have electric blue streaks randomly in her black hair. Between her bright disposition and fluency in both French and Spanish she was set to be their language specialist in the next few years.

"Interesting night last night huh?" she smiled, and for a moment Mandy feared being outted herself. "Sarah must have had a premonition or something, because there's a sub in the Elementary class."

"No, she was just in need of a mental health day. She'd already taken the day off."

"Well, at least the news doesn't know who she is yet."

"I guess that's a good thing."

Therese, Drew's mom, looked at the two of them, and Mandy's face flushed.

"That politician last night? She was talking about our Sarah?"

"Um…well…yes." That killed the conversation pretty quick. Mandy was all about gossip between girls, but not strangers, never strangers.

Mandy filled the fridge with the items purchased for the whole class. A cost saving measure that parents embraced instead of baulked at—buying a week's worth of groceries and cleaning supplies as the classrooms needed. The rotation kept the costs low per family.

The classroom filled with kids and Mandy went to take roll and get them settled into morning learning. Some yawned and Mandy couldn't help but join their sentiment. An evening with Ash usually ended no later than eleven and with a very good night's sleep, but a night with Ash…that doesn't end.

Maybe he was getting all he could since it would be their last time together. Sex with him was just a matter of convenience, not necessity, and definitely not from anyplace where emotions reside. Mandy tamped down what little bit of feelings she had for men years ago. Finding out her best friend's father was hers…well, that kinda nailed it to the floor and there was nothing in her that wanted to pick that bitch up again.

Nine months ago, what little grip she had on the cracked glass ball that was her life had shattered at the news. Mary Beth had the nerve to initially act like it was her fault. Sure, her mom went on dates, but she met them somewhere or she'd go out when Mandy was at a friend's. How was she to know she was in love with Mary Beth's dad? Scratch that, her dad. When she was younger she just assumed he was a great man. The kind of dad she'd like to have. One who you could talk to and who'd welcome her friends into the house. Even as Mary Beth's mother would growl and say nasty things under her breath about Mandy and her mother, Kevin always made her feel worthy.

Mandy went through her day and let the kids distract her. At lunch, she got an orange and string cheese from the fridge. She'd have to remember to restock since normally she brought her own lunch. If Charlie hadn't asked her to eat lunch with him, she'd have snuck out to get fast food.

"Auntie—" Charlie quickly caught himself. "Ms. Mand."

"Yes, Charlie," she said as she sat down on the little chairs at the table that was perfect for the children, but caused her knees to be at her chest.

"Mama's sick lots."

"I noticed that. Are you worried about her?" she asked. Gabbie was still in the first trimester of her pregnancy and hadn't shared the news yet with her kids.

"Uh huh. It's icky." He took a bite of his sandwich, which had been cut into quarters. "I wants to help her."

"Well, what are you doing for her now?"

"I rubs her belly and that makes her smile."

"It sounds like you're doing a lot. Sometimes when we feel bad, just

14

knowing someone loves us can make all the difference."

Charlie set down his piece of sandwich and pondered this comment.

"You know, Ms. Mand, I loves lots of people."

There it was, the simplicity of childhood. Love seems endless and without hesitation. Mandy couldn't remember when her love couldn't be given easily. Charlie had taken to Gabbie the moment they met. Calling her mommy before anyone but he was ready. In this classroom, Mandy had twenty-six students that loved her for her. Unconditionally. As each year passed new ones would have the same reaction. And this love was the only kind she ever wanted.

Chapter Two

"Walking with a friend in the dark
is better than walking alone in the light."
—*Helen Keller*

Ashton had just overstepped the line with the Daughters of Snelling. Thank God Karen was on hyper-vigilant defense mode and not trying to score points or he'd have been in trouble. Normally something like this would have earned him a stern look, a talking to, and an eventual patronizing, if not childish, punishment.

Slashing through the speech on her desk, she seemed different. Stressed, but not. Strange what love can do to a person. Then again, it was more than love, it was…releasing a valve that had been sealed for more than two decades. Hell, maybe three.

"What's the verdict?" Ashton asked.

"I wish I had talked to Sarah before I left this morning."

"Why's that?"

"I think she'd be okay with me naming her, but I'm not sure." Karen rested her head on the palm of her hand. "I asked a woman to marry me."

"You could always throw this back on old Walt somehow."

"No," she sighed. Her eyes seemed to check out for a moment as they glazed over with romance. "She is young though."

"Six years younger, I'm assuming."

"At twenty-four I was in my first campaign and lost to the world."

"So?" he replied and crossed his leg parallel to the floor on his knee. "Sarah doesn't seem to have your learning curve when it comes to life."

Karen arched her eyebrow at Ash, who winked.

The press conference was to be held on the street outside her office to avoid distracting the other offices in the building. Already the pile of local news vans had irritated the offices in the downtown building. Karen liked being close to the capitol instead of buried deep in her constituency. This allowed a bit more leeway with the press. Nestled next to a residential area, the cameras would be under control. Here they could camp out all day.

As they gathered, Ashton could see her searching for Sarah, but alas the woman of her heart was nowhere to be seen. Like the seasoned veteran she was, Karen stepped to the podium and began her apology. Ash stood steadfast as always behind her hoping he wouldn't be part of the question and answer session, but he knew better. Everyone was watching. Friends, family…the RNC. Maybe it was time for him to step from Karen's shadows into another person's. Isn't that what the national committee wanted? Him to put out fires around the party?

"Ash?" Karen turned, and he realized he'd been pondering right over a question. "Would you like to answer the reporter?"

Stumbling thoughts tripped through his mind as he scanned the crowd for one reporter with the most interest on their face. Damn it, they were like kids outside a toy store at Christmas.

"Can I have the question again?"

"What is your involvement in this deceit?" Cynthia, the local Fox reporter, asked.

"That's an ugly word," Ash replied with his signature smirk, and the reporter blushed as well she should. "My best friend was in pain and needed my council and friendship. I couldn't turn my back on her."

"What about the voters? Did you not care that your deception was hurting them?"

"Hurting?" Ashton shifted his stance. "How could it hurt them? I know I'm a catch, Cynthia, but I doubt anyone was caused grievous pain from me being off the market."

"Never assume," Cynthia purred, then caught herself and stepped back.

"Any other questions for me?" Ash asked. He ended up fielding questions from his next step, to whom was he dating in secret. Again Cynthia blushed. Bold little one.

Karen returned to the podium and Ash stood next to Howard in the back and pulled out his phone. Texting Sarah, he hoped for a reply before the end of the press conference. Nothing. Karen began curling her fingers under the podium top, and he knew her tolerance for the same question asked seventy-five ways was wearing thin.

Stepping up after the last question, he nodded to her.

"The Representative has pressing matters, so if there are no further questions," Ash said as he escorted her away while the vultures continued to yell for more.

Karen collapsed in her chair and laid her head on her desk. Sobs cut through him as he tried to tell himself she needed this. She wanted it, but her pain hurt him more than anyone else. For all intents and purposes, she was his sister and no one fucked with his family.

"Get me the number for a new school, Growing Strong Montessori, right now," he ordered his secretary as he went to his desk. The line lit up and he picked up the extension. "Growing Strong Montessori, Mary Beth speaking. How can I help you today?"

"I need to talk to Sarah Lindstrom."

"I'm sorry, Ms. Lindstrom—"

"I don't care that she's in the middle of a class," he snapped.

"I wasn't going to say that," came Mary Beth's harsh reply. He decided to rethink his stance on taking the Growing Strong Mafia head on. "She's not here today."

"What about Mandy?"

"Can I ask who's calling?"

"Ashton Gilmore, Karen's…"

"Oh," she caught herself. "I'll send you through to Mandy's room."

"Thank you."

The phone rang three times and Mandy answered, but her voice was different than he'd ever heard.

"Children's House."

"Mandy?"

"Yes."

"This is Ash. I need a favor."

"I'm working," she said, completely flat.

"Okay, I don't need a favor, Sarah needs one."

"Try again," she groaned. "Remember three strikes, you're out."

"Karen is a mess. I need Sarah to acknowledge her press conference."

"Call her."

Ashton helped himself to a deep, soothing breath. This was so much easier with politicians. "I've been trying."

"She's probably passed out." He heard some movement and muffled voices. Mandy must have put the phone to her chest. Ash's thoughts flipped from concern to desire. Who knew you could want to be a phone receiver. "I'll smack her awake, but Ash, I'm not your beck-and-call girl, so don't expect me to be running around the city for you."

"I know, you're nothing to me, right?" he mocked.

Without hesitation, "nothing at all." The line went dead.

Within twenty minutes Karen had perked up, and Ash patted himself on the back for being the man. Sadly, it was tux time soon. How would schmoozing go with the ménage that was Karen's political life?

Once Sarah arrived, they entered the hotel. The mixed Republican fundraiser had all the candidates milling around. Karen was greeted warmly by the man in charge who shared his own LGBT woes to make a connection that wasn't there. With the normal grace and dignity, Karen smiled and nodded, and then went into a private room and had her meltdown.

Sarah might be able to take his place calming her down. She's done way better than he had in half the time.

"Now what?" Sarah asked as she stood uncomfortably in the gold, satin dress with a small coat after they returned to the party.

"Now," he sighed. "We walk around and share insignificant conversations in an attempt to win votes. If someone has a Walter button you give them an 'aww, isn't it sweet you're supporting the elderly' look."

Sarah covered her lips with her hand as she hid a chuckle.

"It's okay to laugh out loud. Some do it just to get attention."

As if on cue Turner Mueller burst out in an uproarious laugh that cut through the room and caused most to look at the good-natured candidate.

"See."

"But what if someone wants to know what you said?" she asked.

"They won't. They'll just want to be around for the next round of giggles." Ashton placed his hands on Sarah's shoulders and turned her toward Karen, who was shaking hands at a high top table. "Your main job now is to be at her side."

"She wouldn't want to draw attention to herself."

"You're not really to be seen. I'll get you names of people. You're in her shadow. No one notices but her. And see how her neck seems tight and her lips are pursed?"

"Yes," Sarah replied without taking her eyes off Karen.

"When she knows you're there, her whole body is calm." Ashton continued his instruction as he set his replacement on her task. "A slight hand on her mid back will make her melt against you."

"That's always fun," Sarah confessed.

"Go take care of your woman."

With a gentle shove, Sarah crossed the room, and, as he expected, Karen barely looked over her shoulder when Sarah arrived by her side, but her body melted back toward her. Sarah was everything he'd always pretended to be. Bringing a glass of champagne to his lips, he watched the last twenty years of his life slideshow past in a flash. So much time gone and so little to show for it. Without a doubt, it was time to move on. Now for the hard part, deciding what he wanted to do when he grew up.

"Well, if it isn't the man who turns good women to…women," Peter mused as he slapped Ashton on the back. The campaign manager for Walter Thompson had been a pain in Ashton's side for longer than he could remember.

"Your wife did say I was the first man to make her feel like a woman, so I guess you're right."

"Ah, fucking my wife jokes, classic deflection. You should take your act on the road." Peter crossed his arms and raised an eyebrow. "Oh wait. Your candidate isn't going to get past the primary let alone make it to Washington. Guess you're stuck on the local circuit."

"Is it?" Ashton asked, not fazed by the ribbing. "A joke I mean. Karen's going to win, but you may too."

"And how's that?"

"Exactly how far along is your wife?" Ashton gave his best poker face right as Meredith arrived with a huge smile and slightly protruding belly.

"Ashton Gilmore, you better save me a dance," she beamed as her hand glided from his shoulder to his hand where he made sure to hold on, and even took her other hand in his.

"You know you're the only one I step out on Karen for."

"I was so sorry to hear about your breakup. Well, that frees you up for the rest of us, now doesn't it? She didn't know what a good thing she had, did she?"

"Not even once, if you know what I mean," Ashton replied, then winked at Meredith, who blushed red. "She's still my girl, though. I do wish you'd change your vote and support her."

"What I do in the voting booth is none of my husband's business," she said, leaning in close and laughing along with Ash.

Peter's face burned red as he tried to figure a way to grab his wife and get away without causing a scene. It was all about not causing a scene at these damn parties. Snide remarks in the corner followed by innuendo. Ash had become a master. Poor Peter never saw the knight that put him in checkmate.

~ * ~

Mandy tossed her bag on the counter as she flipped on lights. She couldn't remember the last time she came home alone and to an empty house. Silence ate at her and she quickly went to the shower. It was time to reset and refocus. She knew what to do when her home was going away. Roommate and apartment listings on Craigslist would be her night. Well, that and *I Love Rock and Roll*, her new favorite time-and-brain-suck reality show.

Warm water cascaded over her skin and she instantly turned to remove the shower head and adjust it. Sarah could be quite the softy when it came to everything, and Mandy didn't have the time for that. With a flick of her thumb she was violently sprayed with scorching water directly in her face.

"Mother fucking son of a bitch," she screamed, more at herself for being so damn stupid and facing the nozzle toward her face instead of at the drain.

With the shower back in place, she let the sting of heat beat against her skin, penetrating deeper than she'd thought possible. Tangling her fingers in her hair she massaged the shampoo, allowing the hard spray to remove the bubbles. The mixture of soft and hard helped her relax. With her hands flat on the wall in front of her, she gave herself over to the shower.

"I like that moan," a deep voice said. She stood straight up. "Are you using the showerhead for its intended purpose, or have you gone all manual with it?"

"How did you get in my house?" Mandy bit at Ash.

"Sarah needed a change of clothes, she's sleeping at Karen's."

"And?"

"I heard the shower and vulgar language. Knew only one person could be in there."

"Well, you're wrong. I'm with someone and that explained the moan."

"Hmm…" Her panties floated over the top of the shower curtain. "These look more like your size and they're alone."

"He went commando. You know how I hate unwrapping presents."

Mandy stood with the water crashing over her and her arms crossed over her breasts.

"What kind of man wouldn't come out here and kick my ass for being so presumptuous?" Ash asked, and Mandy peeked around the edge of the curtain to see him leaning against the wall holding her salmon colored lace panties out in front of him.

"A naked one."

"So he's threatened by me wearing clothes?"

"Yes, it's not a fair fight."

A moment later a whoosh sounded as Ash pulled the curtain half way and stood in all his naked glory before her.

"Is he in the other half of the tub?" he teased. "That's fucked up. He gets all the water and you get nothing. I'd never do that to you."

Mandy forced herself not to lick her lips or widen her eyes. Worse yet she was not looking down. Not down at the hard pecs that sat above a perfect six pack and that V pointing down.

"Fuck me," she whispered in defeat.

"If you insist." Ash stepped toward the shower, and Mandy stuck her hand out to stop him. "Oh, were you talking to the invisible man in the shower with you?"

Mandy turned off the spray, grabbed a towel from the rack, and wrapped it tightly around her chest.

"Don't you have to bring Sarah her clothes?"

"A car's already brought them over to her house. A few days worth."

"It's the weekend," Mandy growled. "Don't act like it's some big opening for you."

Mandy pushed toward her room as droplets of water streamed down her back and chest from her hair. On her bed was a towel from her last shower and she quickly wrapped her hair up in a turban.

Ashton placed his hands on her shoulders and his lips on her neck the moment they were no longer covered by her hair. Chills raced across her body, perking her nipples, turning the soft fabric of the towel into an irritant.

"Put your clothes on, Ash."

"I feel more comfortable au natural. There's a light airiness to it."

"Much like the wind that blows through your ears."

Defensiveness bit from her lips as his hands slid down her arms. She could feel the heat of his body against her back and when he wrapped his arms around her belly she couldn't explain the sensation. A hug from behind, but it wasn't. She'd expected a hard cock to be pressing against her back. His hands to be pulling at her towel as he bent her over and took her with force. Not unwanted, but the hard and unfeeling sex she was known for. Instead he was touching, softly, lips not sucking hard to create a hickey, but brushing against her skin like one would stroke a rose.

Confusion clouded her mind as she began to fall forward, only to be held tighter by Ash. The smell of his cologne was fresh like soap with a hint of sandalwood. Unknown sensations were like lightning bolts shooting through her body until finally she felt something she knew and understood. Ash tugged at the top of her towel, but he didn't let it drop. Instead he transferred it from her body to his, kissed the back of her neck, then backed away.

"I'll let you get dressed."

When she turned around he was gone.

~ * ~

Ashton plopped on the couch and stretched out. It was a bit colder out here than in the bathroom and damn near iceberg status compared to Mandy's room, but that could have been the company. A throw blanket was laid out on top of the couch, so he pulled it over, rolled on his side, and grabbed his most effective weapon, the remote.

His phone buzzed with a few messages before Mandy walked out in a camisole and pajama pants that on anyone else would mean you ain't getting none of this, but not Amanda Butler. Ash doth think the lady protests too much around him. Although being her sex toy had been fun, he felt ready for an upgrade. Playing the field had also been fun, but nonproductive, and if anything made him a bit jaded about women in general.

Mandy wasn't like women. She was like a dude, he guessed. Not that they were much better. She didn't commit, but he wasn't sure if it was because she didn't want to or couldn't. Wants can change, abilities, on the other hand, those were deeper issues. When she loved, like with her friends, she gave more than herself, and that type of loyalty Ashton understood. That type of loyalty he needed in a lover.

"Comfy?" She snarled while plopping on a chair next to the sofa.

"Getting there," Ashton said as he rolled on his side and rested his head on his palm. "What's on tap for tonight?"

"Why are you here?"

"On the couch? Needed to stretch out."

"In my apartment. Wasn't there a fundraiser tonight?"

"Yes, I raised funds, got supporters, ate bad food, and left my boss with her partner. It's strange not being needed till the end of the night. Guess my social calendar just opened up."

"Too bad you turn women to women."

"Twice in one day…"

"Only twice? You got off easy."

He smiled at the banter. "How was your day?"

"Had lunch with a hot guy. Sadly, a jackass interrupted it."

"Stimulating conversation."

"Better than this," she said as she turned sideways in the chair and flopped her legs over the arm so her head was facing the TV and not him. "Magilla Gorilla, really, why are you here? I had plans tonight."

"Did they include *I Love Rock and Roll*?"

Her head snapped back so fast he feared she may have whiplash, but the lack of cuss words and her glare told him physically she was fine.

"You wouldn't," she snarled as he balanced the remote between his thumb and index finger. It bounced as if he didn't have a tight grip, but when she snapped at it he recoiled and held it tight to his bare chest. "I don't care."

"I heard someone was getting a drink thrown in their face, and then there's hair pulling."

"That's every episode."

Her strange love for bad reality TV with all its staged fights and sudden bursts of anger for no reason in particular confused him. They'd had deep discussions on the world and life in general, and yet she was addicted to TV tripe. She sat pouting with her arms crossed in the chair. When her arm flung wildly, it caught him off guard.

"Are you turning it on or just playing with the buttons?"

"Are you asking about the TV or you?" he challenged, and her whole body moved this time.

"Ashton Archer Gilmore…otherwise known as Aag," she gagged. "What is your purpose in life?"

"I've actually been contemplating that," Ash confessed as he also got out of the comfy position to sit up with the blanket pooled around his waist. Mandy instantly looked at the juncture, and he pulled the blanket up to his chest. "I have eyes you know."

Mandy didn't blush. Instead her hazel eyes with deep brown speckles closed as if she needed the visual break to recover. When their eyes met again she quickly turned away and got up.

"You hungry? I'm starving, although I doubt we have anything substantial."

"Aren't girls supposed to always have healthy food?"

"We've been lax on grocery shopping lately. Kinda distracted by…" she looked around. "Where did you go?"

Ash emerged from the bathroom with his slacks and shirt on,

jingling his keys.

"Let's go."

"No. My hair is wet and I'm in my jammies."

"Jammies?" He smiled. "You surprise me, Amanda. I thought nothing embarrassed you."

"I might see a hot guy there. The last thing I need is to look like I rolled out of bed."

"You don't look like you rolled out of bed. I've seen you when you roll out of bed and right now your face isn't flushed." He stepped closer and stroked her soft cheek. The touch of her had the same reaction he'd felt from the moment he first saw her. Keeping enough of a distance, he continued his seduction. Tonight wasn't about sex. "Your lips are not swollen from being kissed."

"It's not the kissing that swells them." Her voice trembled as she tried to beat him at his own game, but she couldn't play with him either. He could tell she'd never needed, nor wanted, to play with a man. She was used to boys who were excited to have her as a toy. Now she'd have to learn that men treasure works of art. They study them, feel the lines, and become one with them on a level beyond the physical.

"Then what…" His thumb stroked her bottom lip and her eyes glazed over. She no longer seemed to have the ability to turn away from him now. "What makes them swell?"

"Why are you here, Ash?" This time he saw tears pooling in her eyes. Okay, now he was really confused. "I understood before, well, kind of understood, but now you can go on with your life. You don't need to be here."

"Can't I want to?"

"No one *wants* to be with me." Her voice cracked, and he could see her trying to tamp down years of hurt. Twisting in pain, her face tightened as she closed her eyes tightly. He'd broken into a place even the Growing Strong mafia wasn't allowed.

Chapter Three

"The only thing that is constant is change."
—Heraclitius

Mandy never admitted that people didn't want her. To the outside world, she didn't want people. The one thing she knew for sure in life was she didn't know how to make connections. Not the way normal people did. Even though her best friends had never let her down, she feared them leaving every day. Maybe that's why she agreed to buy the daycare center with them so long ago. Then they were contracted to be with her. They couldn't leave.

Ash was confusing the hell out of her right now. He didn't come to fuck. It didn't even seem like he wanted some heavy petting. Outside of turning her on to the point she was aching between her thighs, he seemed to be completely uninterested in anything physical.

"I beg to differ, Amanda," he said, sending a sharp pain to her gut. Amanda…

"If I fuck you will you leave?" she stated plainly.

"Are we doing that again?" he asked and opened the freezer. "I'll admit when you offered a blowjob to get me to turn off CSPAN a few months ago, it was the best exchange I'd ever had, but I'm not really in the mood tonight."

"Since when?"

"Since I realized my life is mine again," he said as he closed the freezer and held a box of frozen taquitos. "And you said you didn't have food. I do have one question for you, though."

"That is?" Mandy asked as she crossed her arms.

27

"What's the deal with the pistachio ice cream? Seriously, there are four cartons in there."

"They were on sale."

"How much can two girls eat?"

"You'd be surprised," Mandy said as she turned on the oven.

Twenty minutes later, they were both sitting on the couch with taquitos, sour cream, and a set of *Smirnoff Ice* drinks watching the latest episode of *I Love Rock and Roll* together.

After eating, Mandy curled her legs underneath her and relaxed against Ash, who had his arm wrapped around her. Snuggled under a blanket she felt the feeling again. The one from before when he just held her. Calm, peace. As his fingers ran through her now dry hair, her muscles relaxed and she felt like she was falling. Comfort and peace were not her thing. She knew something was going to happen. It always did. There was no way a man would just hold her and watch bad TV without—

A frantic knock at her door confirmed her belief in the world. Popping up she rushed to the door as if the person on the other side was bleeding out and she needed to save them. The reality was…just that, her reality.

"Mandy." Her mother's over exaggeration of her name as if she were the only one in the world who could rescue her, grated on Mandy's nerves. Although it did bring her back to her baseline. "Your father has…oh, I can't say it."

Ariel Butler fell into the apartment and noticed Ash sitting on the couch. Thank God he was still fully dressed.

"I'm sorry to interrupt," she said as she held tightly to Mandy's hands. "I only need her for a moment, and then you two can go back to your date."

"It's not a date," Mandy coolly replied.

"Oh, honey, no need to introduce me. I know how those early dates are."

"It's not a date," Mandy repeated. "What's wrong?"

"He's never going to leave her."

After twenty-five-years her mother still didn't have a clue.

"Maybe I should leave," Ash said as he stood. "This seems like a private conversation."

"Let me lay it out for you. This is my mom, Ariel. She's been dating Mary Beth's father for…let's just say prior to my conception. You remember Mary Beth, right?"'

"Yes." Ash nodded and seemed uncomfortable for the first time ever. Mandy smiled. 'Bout time.

"She's my sister, did you know that?"

"I'm not sure…" he said as he shifted back and forth.

"Don't feel bad, I've only known for a few months too. Or has it almost been a year? Time does fly."

Her mother glared at her. Not because of sharing the secret. That she could care less about. The more who knew the better in her mind. She was pissed because Mandy wasn't paying attention to her major problem that was a quarter of a century old.

"Mandy, please, your friend doesn't want to get caught up in your childish whining. It isn't an attractive quality for a woman."

Mandy rolled her eyes, then rested against the wall.

"See ya, Ash," Mandy said. Ash didn't wait for her to change her mind as he took off. "So, Mom, Dad's an asshat who prefers his dying wife to you?"

"Quit taking her side. Between having kids and cancer she's kept that man by her side for too long. Why would you want to be with a man who's in love with someone else?"

"I have no idea," Mandy patronized her mother who went on for the next hour about Kenneth Wallace and his undying love for her.

Crawling in bed after sending her mother home, Mandy stared at the ceiling and wondered for the final time that day. What the hell had Ashton Gilmore been doing in her house?

~ * ~

"This is the final push." Howard's red face and clenched fist shook. Ash looked at him and wondered if one or both might fall off. "Over the next seventy-two hours it's make or break with this campaign. We've had a major setback."

"I'm assuming that's me," Karen whispered in Ash's ear, and he chuckled under his breath.

"But we can overcome it. Our foundation is solid, whereas Walter Thompson's has yet to set even after fifty years of being loyal to the party. He thinks it's his time." Howard was building up to his largest statement. "But it is ours. The time of Karen Schroeder to lead the Republican Party into the future. Breaking ceilings of gender and now sexual…"

Karen tapped Ash's shoulder and the two of them stepped from the back of the room to the small desk he had behind a cubical wall.

"I can't listen to more," she sighed and placed her head on the desktop. "I'm all right with everyone else, but something about Howard discussing sexual preference…"

"At least he doesn't know about your bondage fetish," Ash teased.

"Where were you last night? I was talking to a county commissioner, then I looked away and you were gone."

"Sarah needed someone to grab some clothes and I was getting tired. Wasn't it nice to just go home after the meeting and not need to make stops?"

"I guess." Karen gave him a puzzled look, and then they were interrupted by Kimberly.

"Sorry," she apologized as she fumbled with a stack of books and papers. "You guys still sneaking off together?"

"I keep trying to convince her my kiss causes deeper trembles, but she won't believe me," he replied and winked at Kimberly as he sat on the edge of the desk. "Maybe we could go somewhere and you could tell me if I kiss better than a woman."

"Or, you could shut your pie hole before I get a sexual harassment case filed," Karen snapped and took the top stack of papers from Kimberly.

"I don't mind," she cooed a bit, and Karen smacked Ash's back when he leaned closer. "Right, well, Howard has everyone fired up and the phone bank starts in a few minutes. These are the latest talking points that need your approval."

"How much has changed from last time?" Karen asked right as Kimberly's grip started to slip and Ash caught the box on the bottom of the pile and set it to the side.

"Thanks." She smiled, and Ash thought it'd be so easy to take this to the next level, and by level that meant little more than her against a wall somewhere. He was surprised to find he didn't want that.

"So, Karen," he said as he turned away from the aid and focused on his job. Even Karen was surprised by his turn. "Anything you don't like?"

"Um, Kim, can we get a few minutes?" Karen asked and watched as Kim backed out of the area. "I've been lost in myself lately. What's going on with you?"

"Being your best cheerleader."

"Ash, Kim offered herself to you on a platter."

"Not hungry."

"A few days ago, you were complaining about not getting laid."

Ash stood silent.

"She must be amazing if you're turning someone down."

"I can't focus on anything but my Kare Bear."

Really he couldn't think past Mandy's curves. Flashes of her dark hair streaming down her back as she arched while riding his hips. Remembrance of the way her breasts felt when he cupped them as he pulled her closer. The taste of her neck as her hair fell to the side, exposing the skin to his lips. Backward…reverse cowgirl…Mandy had taught him positions he thought only existed in ancient texts.

~ * ~

"The next time you send the errand boy to fetch for you, how about a warning?" Mandy bit out the moment she saw Sarah on Monday morning.

Blinking her eyes a few times, she blew on her coffee, took a drink, and then set it down.

Sarah glanced over at Gabbie, who'd taken a keen interest in the conversation, before responding. "Morning, Ms. Mand, and how are you today?"

"I'd be a lot better if Friday night I could have taken a shower alone."

"I thought you liked showering in groups of two or three," Sarah retorted.

"Again, one time," snapped an exasperated Mandy. "I thought you were gone."

"You asked me to join."

Mandy caught herself, and then shifted her angry stance. She'd forgotten that time.

"It was two girls. You needed to move on from Lisa."

"There was another time, wasn't there?"

"That's not the point," Mandy said without truly answering. "The point was when I shower with someone I ask them there, they don't just show up."

"Charlie and mees takes baths together." Claire had found her way into the teacher's lounge.

"Charlie and I," Gabbie corrected.

"You too?" Claire asked wide eyed. "He must be really stinky."

"No." Gabbie shook her head, and then gave up on the correction. Instead she passed her daughter a banana. "Claire, I think you need to head back to the care room."

"K, mama, bye aunties."

Claire skipped out of the lounge, and Gabbie gave Mandy a scowl.

"This is not my fault," Mandy whined.

"It isn't?" Gabbie challenged.

"No," Mandy said with all the surety of one of her students. "It's Sarah's."

"Now when I said I'd be the principal I knew I'd have to handle the occasional disagreements between children that escalated to me. As a teacher, I knew I would, but never did I imagine I'd have a finger pointing contest between my staff."

"Oh please," Sarah scoffed. "You knew you would."

"Okay, but it's not really easy to do this with you two."

"Do what?" Mandy asked.

She pointed to Claire skipping down the hall. "Discussions need to be G rated."

"How about students aren't allowed in the teacher's lounge just because they're related to the principal?" Mandy suggested. "And you don't know what she did."

"Okay, what did Sarah do?" Gabbie's patronizing tone grated against Mandy's tired, frayed nerves. "Use your words."

"Frick both of you." Mandy began to storm out when Gabbie stepped in the doorway and pointed to the small, round table in the center of the room. "Forget it, I was wrong, she's perfect."

"Turn around."

"Fine." With a pout, Mandy plopped in the chair and crossed her arms.

"Really, I don't care, but don't bring it in here," Gabbie said.

"She gave her key to the man I hate more than air."

"You hate air?" Sarah chided.

"Why would you send Ash to *our* apartment?"

"He offered."

"I'm sure he did," Mandy sneered.

"It's not like he was going to stay, he just ran in and grabbed some clothes for me."

"Did you miss the part about me showering alone?"

"He got in the shower with you?"

"Well…no…" Mandy suddenly had two sets of eyes on her and the last thing she wanted was to admit that she and Ash were anything but mortal enemies. "He came in the bathroom and scared the crap out of me. If my mom hadn't showed up, I'd have been stuck with him all night."

"Why wouldn't he leave?" Sarah asked as if Mandy were lying.

"Because his goal in life is to torture me with his smell."

"He didn't do that thing where he lifts his arm and chases you around with his pit?" Gabbie asked.

"No—it's just—who would—you know what? Never mind. From now on I'll just leave the key to our apartment taped to the door. That way anyone can come in."

"I'm sorry. You're right. I shouldn't have just given Ash the key. He's like Karen's brother. I don't think of him as a guy."

"You don't think of anyone as a guy. It was totally not cool."

"You're right," Sarah said as she took another sip of coffee. "I know he irritates you, but I wish you two could get along."

"You know what? I just need a night out."

"We're hopefully having a party tomorrow night at Karen's campaign headquarters."

"Wow…um…let me see, no." Mandy glared at Sarah who shrugged her shoulders and placed her lunch in the break-room fridge.

Mandy headed to her classroom, tucking away her phone on the top shelf of her supply closet. Right as she set it down it buzzed. Retrieving it, she read the text and rolled her eyes.

Hey, Mandy, need a favor, Ash.
I'm working.
Not hard.

She blanched. Of course he wouldn't think she actually did something. Typical.

Take a blue pill and make sure it doesn't last for more than four hours.

You're responding to my texts so you couldn't be working too hard.

Oh sure he wants to be a grown up.

I'm putting my phone away.

I need a favor on Friday.

Mandy sighed and had to give Ash credit for not asking her to rush out in the middle of her day.

I work Friday.

8 at night?

Eight on Friday night…this fool was not trying to ask her out.

Ash, I'm not going on a date with you.

Hurt as I am, I wasn't asking you out.

Mandy felt a sting on her face as if she'd been slapped.

"Hey, Mandy," Jasmine said as she walked into the closet, making Mandy jump. "Sorry."

"You're just really quiet." Mandy's phone was making a bubble popping sound to indicate Ash was still typing.

I need a ride.

Oh, so you want to fuck me, just not take me to dinner first. Thanks, but no thanks.

Again…no…

Ash sent another rapid fire text.

Am I just sex to you?

Not even that. You were a time suck.

There was some sucking…a lot of sucking, but about the ride I need.

My class is coming in I have to go.

Mandy placed her phone on the top shelf still hearing the bubble popping sound. She could hold off learning what he wanted. Smiling, she closed the closet door, only to have the phone buzz. Her hand curled around the handle and she had to breathe out. A vice clenched in her stomach. Why did she care? Shaking out her hands she walked to her observation stool and took roll as the kids came into the room, each greeting her in their individual ways. Mandy's leg was bouncing as she wondered about that last text message.

The gorilla couldn't want anything really important. If he did, her classroom phone would be ringing. Ten minutes of wondering was the most she could handle. Practically leaping from the small stool, she ran over little Harrison and had to apologize. What the hell was the matter with her? Running over a student for a man. She didn't think about men at work. Men, sex, her fucked up life—that was for when she wasn't in the safety of Children's House.

"I'm so sorry, Harrison," she said as she knelt by the four-year old.

"'tis okay, Ms. Mand, sometime I gotta go potty really bad too."

She smiled and ruffled his hair. "You're a pretty cool kid."

"I know," he said then skipped over to the puzzle rack.

When she stood, Jasmine was giving her a quizzical look. Shaking her head, she went to the closet and retrieved her phone.

Need a ride…to the airport freakzilla.

I don't do airports.

She replied and stashed the phone, making sure to block out any beeping or buzzing noises.

Chapter Four

"Do the right thing. It will gratify some people and astonish the rest."
—Mark Twain

I don't do airports.

Ash's phone buzzed on the table in the conference room, causing the strategy team to turn and look at him. It's not like they'd been told to turn off their phones. It was Howard who was the most interested. Had he heard about the RNC's offer? He must have. Ashton looked around the table and could feel the disconnect. Whether Karen wins or loses tomorrow, he no longer had a place in this room. Had he ever?

"Ash, something you want to share with the group?" Howard grumbled.

"Not particularly?"

"Anything you'd like to add to the conversation?"

"Why are we even discussing tomorrow's election?" he asked. "She's going to win. We need to think further ahead."

"I'm glad you're so certain," Karen nervously said as her thumb repeatedly clicked her pen. "I've alienated a huge chunk of my voters."

"This is a primary, Kare. Not only do the voters need to be preregistered with a party to vote, but they need to actually show up. We all know the statistics."

"Right, this is a primary." Karen slapped the pen down on the table. "Which means informed voters will be going and I've been all over the damn news."

"Name recognition. Come on, the days of people studying the

candidate are over. It's all about flash and who was on the news last. Half the people aren't even paying attention to the news in the background."

"Thanks for your insight, but how about you let the grownups handle this," Howard interjected. Ash waited for Karen to stick up for him, but she kept quiet.

"I have to fluff my hair anyway." Ash pushed back from the table and left.

What does 'you don't do airports' mean? Are you afraid to fly? Because I'm the one flying...

Sending the text, Ashton pulled up his email and reread the itinerary for his trip. He'd be meeting with a handful of senators who would need to amp up their campaigns in the next few years. Talk with two campaign managers and have dinner with the chair and vice chair of the RNC. For someone not big enough to sit at the grownup table, the rest of the world seemed to be licking their chops to have him. They saw him as the next bright political mind, according to Victor.

The meeting broke up, and Karen popped by his cubical.

"Sorry about that."

"Karen, when you're elected, where do I fit in?"

"I love that you believe so much in me."

"That must be nice," he said and took her lack of response not as a slight and not caring, but frazzled nerves.

Five hours later, Mandy finally responded.

I don't take people to airports and I never pick them up.

Wouldn't that be two nevers, then?

There are people I'll drop at the airport if I really want to go to the Mall of America and it's on my way.

She certainly was typing back a lot for telling him no. The corners of his mouth twisted up a bit.

I see. Eight at night...you can't go shopping.

That and I hate you.

The fact you keep fucking me makes me forget. Thanks for the reminder.

Anytime Magilla.

Karen didn't need him and Mandy's too busy pretending she hates him. Only one solution. Alcohol and pool.

Ash wasn't one to get drunk and even if he'd lost his formal duties he knew there were some things Karen would need tomorrow. Despite his desire to find a bar and see if he was capable of emptying its stock, he'd have to find another way to while away the hours tonight.

The Triple Crown Batting Cages would have to be his answer. In the trunk of his car were his bats since less than a week ago, he'd been playing softball with Mandy and the rest of her friends, ironically at the field next to the cages.

Rounding the corner, he looked for the first open slot, only to see he'd been beaten to his thinking spot by the very same dark haired temptress who'd caused half of his frustration. A loud thwack reverberated off her metal bat as she swung, then returned to her stance, only to whiff on the next ball.

"You know what's wrong?" Ashton observed. She missed the next ball, but that one was his fault.

"That you have no concept of a one-night-stand," she retorted, and then swung and missed. This time she smashed her bat against the ground before resetting herself.

"How many did you miss before I got here?"

With a whirr the machine let another one loose and Mandy's bat made contact with a slight tick, sending the ball straight up in the air. She stepped to the side and let it drop before she kicked it away.

Ash went into his own cage and unloaded his quarters into the machine. Flipping a few bats in his hand until he found the one he wanted, a Louisville Slugger he got freshman year, he got in his stance and looked at Mandy across from him. Being a switch hitter was paying off as he settled into his stronger side, the left. With a crack of wood, the ball sailed into the netting above the cage and he smiled. Mandy glared at him as she stood ready to hit. Ash didn't take his eye off her when a flash of white caught his peripheral vision and he swung, hitting the ball perfectly while still staring at Mandy, who completely missed the ball that crashed into the back of the cage.

"You suck."

"Not unless prodded," he replied and hit another ball to the back wall.

"Fine, what am I doing wrong?" she asked with her arms spread. "And I swear to God if you say anything about choking up on the bat…"

Ash hit pause on his machine, used his bat as a third leg, and crossed his right foot in front of his left to balance it on the toe.

"Your hands are not the problem." He smirked a bit. "You can hold a bat with the best of them."

"I swear Ash—" She pointed her bat at him.

"Your hips."

Mandy dropped the bat and turned her head to inspect her ass…again, not the problem.

"When you're in your stance they aren't parallel to the base. Has anyone ever said you had an ugly hit, but at least it's effective?"

"And if they did?"

"It's your hips. Seriously woman. It's the same when you're having sex."

"Now you're complaining about that?"

"No man really complains, but I have a feeling you've pinched a guy or two in your day."

Mandy turned around, then stepped toward the fencing shared by their cages.

"What is your problem with how I fuck?"

"No real connection." Her face paled. "It was probably because it was only a one-night-stand, but there's more than one position."

"I think I've shown you my flexibility."

"I guess." He stepped back and poked the start button on his machine. Mandy hadn't moved. Settling his hips and feet he stared down the ball and another loud thwack sent the ball a bit right for him.

"You're not that flexible, you know. I bet you couldn't even—"

Ashton crossed the distance so fast Mandy jumped. He curled his fingers around her hands and kept her trapped with only the metal fencing between them. His heart pounded as he made sure to be just gentle enough to not scare her, but still be firm.

"If you looked past your annoyance of me I have a feeling you and I could be very good friends. Even more." Her eyes widened and her lips parted slightly. "You don't let anyone close, do you? Not once."

"I did once." Her breath quickened, and he could see she was straining to look away, but couldn't find the strength.

"What happened?"

"She married someone else."

~ * ~

Ash's warm fingers released from Mandy's and cold tore up her arms, settling in her heart.

"Oh," Ash sighed and turned around. This time, when he hit the ball, it was from the right.

"You're a switch hitter?" She awed.

"Seems popular today." The second ball pulled a bit to the left, but still would end up in the outfield.

"Show me…" she began, unsure why. He'd obviously been disgusted by her comment. "With my hips."

"You know everything anyway."

"Seriously?" she spat. "You're upset about me being in love with a woman."

Ash turned and smashed his bat against the gate. "I've spent the last ten years being a lesbian's beard and finding sex in random places. That I did because, like you, I fell in love with a woman who could never love me. The last thing I'm about to do is repeat the same mistake."

"I'm not gay, and I'd never be in the closet if I was."

"Lucky me." A ball whizzed behind him and crashed against the gate. "Are there any women that like men anymore?"

"Please, Ashton, you get laid like the world was made of tile. The last thing you should be bitching about is a few lesbians."

"So what are you then?"

"In particular."

"Man, woman, beast?"

"I draw the line at beast, but if I'm attracted to someone I'm not going to stop."

"Even if you hate them."

She smiled, crossed her arms, and turned away.

"Even if I hate them more than air." Her voice was distant even to herself.

"How do you hate air?"

"It's a saying," she groaned.

"I don't think so, I think you want it to be a saying...but no one is saying that."

"Look here, Magilla, are you going to handle my hips or let your quarters keep smashing against the gate?" A few balls had flown past him during their fight.

"You have any left?"

"Yep."

When Ash came into Mandy's cage she watched him with his wife beater on. He'd obviously just come from work and didn't have any gym clothes with him. Instead he wore baseball cleats, dress pants, and his undershirt.

Standing behind her, he placed his hands on her hips and she tried to focus on the ball, not how good it felt to have his large hands gripping her hips tightly. She couldn't force herself to turn away, so she scrunched her eyelids shut to block him out. She heard him go over and smack the start button, and then steadily advance on her. Leaning close, she could feel his warm breath on her neck and her skin erupted.

"Open your eyes," he whispered, and she fluttered her eyes, not even noticing they were closed. The sense of sight seemed useless compared to the exhilaration of touch at the moment. "Bend just a bit and look at the machine."

The ball rolled from the bottom to the top as the large, gray wheel spun. With a gust of wind, the ball came flying toward her and she swung her arms. Her bat made contact with the ball and the line drive would have taken out any pitcher.

Ash's hands hadn't moved even when her hips strained against it.

"Next time swing up a bit," he ordered, and she resettled herself.

Ten swings later, with only one miss, Ash had finally backed off, but his grip had left a mark on her hips. She was sure of that. On the first few swings when he no longer held tightly she slipped a bit, but was able to reset quickly. When she turned, Ash had his left hand above his head and fingers curled around the fencing. A peek of skin exposed his own hip a bit. Taking a step toward him her fingers glided across his skin, but he didn't drop his hand. Instead he let her run her fingers under his shirt as he stayed extended against the fence.

"Thanks for the tip," she purred.

"You're just lucky I watch your ass."

She smirked. "Why are you here, Ash?"

"I've had a fucked up day and needed to regroup. And you?"

"The same."

"How 'bout grabbing a beer and talking about our plight?"

"I could eat. How about Newman's in North St. Paul? It's just up the road."

They drove separate cars, but Ash followed her and she could see his face in her rearview mirror. Downtown North St. Paul kept its small town feel even as the Twin Cities grew around it. The two-block strip of downtown has four bars, antique shops, a used book store, and barber shop among its other small stores. Newman's owns the claim to the longest running bar in Minnesota. Even telling the tale of how it served meals in the front and liquor in the back during prohibition. Monday nights were dollar burger night and the place was a bit packed. Perfect in Mandy's mind. The constant chaos could keep her distracted enough to not focus on Ash too much.

Grabbing a high top table, they ordered a few baskets of fries and burgers. To her surprise, Ash ordered a Grain Belt while she became the hipster ordering the local Nordeast.

"What made your day shitty?" she asked while they waited for their food.

"Can you keep a secret?"

"What is it with you and Karen? Is there anything that's transparent about you?"

"I'm sorry, how many of your friends know we've been together?" Mandy crossed her arms and arched her eyebrow.

"Guess I can keep a secret then."

"I was offered a job in DC."

"That's cool, but aren't you going there anyway?"

He shook his head. "Karen needs to win the primary and general. She also has to decide if I'm going to be on her team when she goes."

"Why wouldn't she bring you? Haven't you worked for her forever?"

"As window dressing. I've noticed lately that she doesn't need to hide behind me, and she's not consulting me on anything." Ash ran his hand over his face. "I didn't think we were actually breaking up when she asked Sarah to marry her. We were friends first, but now...I have no idea what I am to her."

"Still her bestie, I assume. It's not like you ever had benefits anyway." The food arrived and Mandy popped a few hot fries in her mouth. She instantly regretted her impulsiveness.

"I used to be someone to whom she turned for guidance."

Mandy set her elbow on the table and rested her chin on her palm. "This job in DC, what would you do?"

"Guide. Help others hide who they really are or whatever dirty deeds they've committed."

"They see you as an expert, I suppose."

He shrugged. "Yeah, it's just temporary until I can get in with a lobbying company."

"That your longterm goal? Lobbying?"

"Right now, I'm not one for political office, but I love the hum."

"Why couldn't you run? You've got the smile, voice, and I assume the pedigree. Or are you a mutt?"

"Not a mutt in the traditional sense of the word. Years of seeing Karen binge on antacids never appealed to me."

"But she was lying about who she was."

Ash sat silently in contemplation for a moment, and Mandy wished she could read him like she could her friends. The moment they entered a room she could tell their every thought and what they had been doing since they were last together. Ash was a mystery.

"You never lie do you?" he asked.

"I suppose I do, everyone does, but I've not found it very useful."

"But you don't, not about the big things. You also don't apologize for what you are."

Mandy glared at him as fire burned up her throat. "What exactly am I?"

"You tell me. I can't think of a time when you've shown shame…except maybe about me," he said as his eyebrow rose. "Why is that?"

Pain seared her chest as he looked at her for an explanation she couldn't give. He was right. She didn't lie. If she wanted someone, she didn't mess around playing stupid games. Most men couldn't handle the fact she asked them out…although being forward enough to ask for sex never seemed to deter them. With women, they loved how she took control of a situation they weren't ready to deal with in the first place half the time.

"You seriously don't like me, do you?" he asked.

Mandy felt her face flush. "No. How could I like someone like you?"

"Why did your day suck?"

"Besides you showing up and ruining my quiet time?"

"It sucked before then or you wouldn't have needed your smashy time."

"You have a point and you didn't totally ruin my day." Mandy pushed a fry around in her ketchup. "I've had a f'd up year."

"What started it?"

"Gabbie got married."

A look of realization spread over Ashton's face. "You're in love with Gabbie."

"In the only way I can love someone, I suppose. I can talk to her, or I could. She never judged me. See, Mary Beth's mother hated me, and although Mary Beth would stick up for me, she's a bit judgy."

"What about Sarah?" Ash queried.

"She's Mary Beth's best friend. They knew each other long before the rest of us. She grew to love me, but Gabbie's different."

"Gabbie's happy, right?"

Mandy took a long drink from her beer before reflecting. "Blissfully, it's sickening really, but I'd been holding a torch I guess. Misspent youth and all."

"Being in love isn't misspent time."

"Says the beard of the news's favorite politician," Mandy chided.

"I fell in love with her," he confessed at his own misspent youth. "But I'm not in love with her. That ship sailed years ago."

Mandy eyed him, scanning his brain searching for lies. He stayed steadfast and she hated his calm.

"Gabbie's been with her husband a while now right?" he asked.

"Yes."

"Okay, what happened next in the Amanda Butler year of pain and punishment?"

"You met my mother." Mandy bit her hamburger and allowed herself to settle before that tale started.

"Briefly. That was the whole Mary Beth's my sister thing?" Mandy nodded as she finished chewing. "How exactly did that work?"

"My mom was eighteen and in my dad's office. I guess Grace was pregnant with Mary Beth and it freaked him out. At least that's the story I got. My mom got preggers and our dad decided he needed to stay with Grace."

"Okay, but how did you not know?"

"They kept the affair quiet. According to my mom every time she had dad ready to marry her, Grace got pregnant."

"By herself, that's a bit hard to believe."

"My point exactly." Mandy's hands flew up in the air. "You get it. She's forty-three and doesn't get it. I swear I could've figured this one out when I was eighteen, but not my mom."

"And he never told you?"

"Nope, I thought my mom had been knocked up by some rock star or something and never got over him. For a while I believed he was dead."

"Damn."

"Kevin was always nicer to me than the other girls, but I thought it was because Grace was such a bitch. Now I get it. I look just like my mom."

"A walking reminder and her daughter's best friend. That had to be hard."

"Really, both of our mothers are morons. Grace had five kids trying to keep him when he wasn't going anywhere and my mom gave up chances with a good guy for the dream that is my father."

"You sure he only has two families?"

"You joke, but no. I can't trust anything he says. Even now he won't let us tell the younger kids. Only Mary Beth knows. Her sister Jillian loves to hang out with me…the only sisters I've had were my friends and now I have three and two brothers, only we can't talk about it."

"And you don't lie about the big things," Ash said with awe. "I knew you were strong, but you impress me."

"What, my repressed rage?"

"It's been bubbling up." Ash waved at the waitress to get them a second round.

"I guess. You're not helping."

"I'm not?" Ash asked as if he'd been wounded. "I was sure I was releasing tension in your body."

"My feelings for you are messing with my head."

"The thin line of love and hate?"

"The blur of trust and the real world."

"Amanda," he said as he placed his hand over hers and stroked the back with his thumb. A shiver shot up her spine and every sound was drowned out except for his voice. "You can trust me."

Sincerity oozed from his lips, and she wanted to believe in Ash. It'd be easy. They'd all be paired up and could have those stupid parties Gabbie seemed to be planning all the time. Couples all gathered with children and a barb-b-q. Only that wasn't her experience. It wasn't her life and Ash would leave like all the rest.

"You're going to DC anyway," Mandy said with a smile as tears stung her eyes.

"It sounds like we're both trying to find a place in the world," he observed and took her hand in his.

His thumb stroked her knuckles, sending heat up her arm. Gentle, yet firm. The line he used could be in a trashy romance novel or *Lifetime* movie where she'd ridicule it while throwing popcorn at the TV. Instead she felt herself falling for his words mixed with his touch. His left hand reached for her. As he cradled her cheek in it they met in a slow and sensual embrace. Firm lips softened as they parted and his tongue found hers just as eager to enter his mouth as she was to have him in hers. Eyes closed once again. Touch was the only sensation she wanted.

Ashton Gilmore had to have the most talented mouth on the planet, next to hers. It took every ounce of control she had to not crawl on his lap and slowly ride what had to be a hard cock at this point. Her hand glided up his thigh. She'd almost reached him when they were rudely interrupted.

"Careful there, lady," a man said as he touched her back with what might as well of been a spike. "You're kissing him now, but you'll probably end up with Sasha by the end of the night."

Mandy's teeth clenched as she turned, already about to kill the man touching her. The insult just put her over the edge. At five-ten and a minimum of two-fifty, asshole supreme had a three-day old version of a five o'clock shadow. Or he would if there weren't random patches of little to no growth.

"Let me guess, you can satisfy me?" she growled while trying to determine if his faded shirt was actually from a championship he'd been a part of or just some crap he cheered for in nineteen eighty-six.

"A hell of a lot better than he can," he offered with a crooked smile while running his fingers through his brown hair.

"Let's go," Ash said as he tossed money on the table.

"Run away, pussy. No wonder your girlfriend left you for a woman. She needed someone with balls."

"Guess that kept you out of the running," Ash bit and pulled on Mandy's arm, but she didn't move. She couldn't. It was animalistic the way she was when it came to attacks on her friends. Who knew Ash qualified?

"Whatever, Ashley…isn't that your name, Ashley?"

The whole knee to the crotch was so played out, but Mandy did love the classics. Only the man didn't crumple to the floor, his face didn't redden, and better yet all she got was a sharp intake of air. Mandy laughed as she kept her hands on the man's shoulders because he barely reacted.

"You're right, Ash, he is out of the running."

~ * ~

The mixture of desire and need to man up for himself swirled in Ash. He expected the shit he'd been getting, but to have a woman be forceful about protecting him? He was unsure of that. Shouldn't he be knocking this guy into next week? But then again Mandy had just nullified the web-toed children he might produce if he was able to slip a date rape drug into someone's drink.

Mandy's smile had desire winning. As a man, his normal reaction to the vision of a nut crushing action was to at least wince in pain, but all he could see were her hazel eyes dancing in the little light streaming in from outside. The way her full lips curled in utter joy. She was having fun.

"Having a girl fight for you—"

"I'm more than willing to fight you outside, I'm just waiting for your Cro-Magnon brain to register you getting kicked in the nuts," Ash said, a bit incredulously. "You do have a sack, right?"

"She doesn't kick that hard."

"Yes…yes, she does," Ash assured him, even though he'd never been on the receiving end, he knew Mandy well enough. The fight and vigor turned him on more than the kiss. Taste and feel were nothing like seeing her in action.

"What, she drag you around by them?"

Ash questioned how drunk this guy had to be. Questions pertaining to his manhood he'd been expecting for years. Even his dad gave him a queried looked when he first discussed Karen. Truthfully, Ash didn't expect it to last as long as it had. But that's how it was with lies—unless cut off they will overgrow like crabgrass.

"Look," Ash leaned in. "Asshole. I'm just trying to have a nice meal with my friend here."

"She friend zoned you." He chuckled and hitched his thumb at Ashton, almost hitting his face. "This fucktard can't get out of the friend zone with a girl. The least you could've got was to watch the girls, that is unless that's not something you're interested in."

"You offering?" Ashton asked as he waved his hand. "It would explain your obsession with my balls."

"Now that's something I'd watch," Mandy said as she slid her hand down Ash's pants and wrapped her hand around his manhood. "You bent over with him slamming into your ass. You wouldn't walk right for a week. Take it from someone who knows."

"Okay, all of you out," the bartender said, finally entering the situation a bit too late.

"Your hand," Ash gulped as his lips brushed Mandy's ear.

"Is full."

"True, but..." Mandy stroked up and Ash clenched from lips to asshole.

"And very comfortable."

"I agree, but I'm not sure we're in the right place for it."

In resignation Mandy sighed and retracted her hand.

"Actually, that I was a bit jealous of," the bartender said as he winked at Mandy. "But I need you guys to head out."

They turned to see two police officers standing on either side of the door with their hands resting on their duty belts. They both bore a slightly intimidating pose with looks as dark as their uniforms.

"We good here, Terry?" the one on the right asked.

"I think so...Pete, just met someone who could shut his trap." The bartender pointed toward the guy who'd wrecked their dinner.

"The guy or the girl?" the one on the left asked.

"Hard to say, they're both smartasses."

"Pete, I don't know why they let you in this place," the left one said.

"Mom says I have to," Terry whined.

"Not tonight, head on out," the one on the right said as he scanned the three of them.

Pete grumbled as he pushed past the two cops, but Mandy made sure to make a spectacle of herself as she clung to Ash while they walked out.

"I can't believe you molested me in a bar," Ash laughed from deep in his gut.

"You're right, it should be done in a dark place with no witnesses."

"Says the nursery school teacher."

"Children's House."

"Munchkins all." Ash wrapped his arms around Mandy and spun her. "You have no filter, do you?"

"I never saw a need for one."

Ash brushed back Mandy's dark hair and gazed into her hazel eyes with deep chocolate speckles. He saw something he'd never seen before. Vulnerability. Sex with Mandy tonight would be more than just the physical, and she was petrified. He'd broken her, and he wasn't sure if that's what he meant to do. She was still strong, but what she offered tonight wasn't her body. He knew she'd be offering herself. Crushing his lips against hers, he held her head in his hands, knowing they couldn't do more. Mandy wasn't ready for what he had to offer. Moreover, he wasn't sure if he could give all of himself. Not until he knew where his life was going.

"I want to spend the night with you," he whispered against her lips.

"Kinda figured that out," she purred as her hands came from behind him and pulled at his shirt.

He grasped them and stopped her.

"I want to spend the night with you," he repeated, making sure to keep his eyes on her. "I want to hold you and have you in my arms when I wake up in the morning."

Mandy stepped back and looked both ways down the sidewalk as if he'd asked to tie her to a lamppost, slather her in honey and lick every inch of her body while people watched. Strangely she'd probably not have hesitated as much with that request. He intertwined their fingers. Mandy acted as if the mere gesture was foreign to her and perhaps it was. Karen had loved the feeling of every nook being protected, but not held tightly.

"Who's loved you?" he asked.

"Many," she responded defensively. "And none all in the same breath."

"Then they were fools."

"They were not allowed," she stated plainly and took another step back. Her fingers trailed from his slowly. Fear of breaking the connection mixed with the knowledge she'd needed this too. He'd seen her vulnerability and chosen right. "If we do this I need to go slow. Like a turtle crawling in molasses unsure of which way to turn slow."

"Thinking it's going to try to back up?" he added.

"I've done a lot of things over the years," she confessed.

"Exposed…"

She trailed off and looked to the side once again.

"I'm not really the monogamy hero I play on TV either."

She chuckled, but kept her head down.

"There is one thing…" Rocking back on her heels she let out a long gust of air. "You know how to keep secrets."

"Will you take me to the airport?" he asked.

"Not even if the fate of the free world depended on it."

Mandy had to say she'd waken up in worse conditions than next to a half-dressed Ashton Gilmore. In fact, she'd rather enjoyed the softness of his skin and the warmth of his body. Three in the morning and she didn't know what to do. They'd watched a movie and he'd held her. At first, she twisted and turned unable to get comfortable, but slowly as the night wore on her body, she grew tired and could no longer fight it. She knew she'd passed out on the couch and having been moved to a whole other room should have sent her into panic mode upon waking. Instead she snuggled closer and nestled into the crook of his shoulder.

Not waking, his hand stroked against her bare shoulder, and then pulled her in tightly. The spiced smell of his body made her mouth and other parts water, but he wasn't here for that. He was here for her. They'd spent the night in light discussions at first, and then they went deeper. Mandy kept her distance, though. He could bare his soul all he wanted—hers would stay where it belonged, locked away in a room no one could breech.

The second time she woke her bed was still warm, but empty. If it weren't for the voice coming from the other room she would have assumed Ashton had made the same choice all the rest had. The fragrance of coffee crept along the air like the veil of a belly dancer. Would following it be a tease, or was the dark goddess of warmth and brain power actually dwelling in her kitchen?

"Love you, Kare," Ash said, hanging up the phone and placing it on the counter. His broad smile appeared when he turned and saw Mandy on the other side. "Ninja skills, you warned me."

"I can kill a man with my pinkie toe," she teased and worked her way around to the coffee pot.

"It's so cute and adorable, though." He kissed the back of her neck, but she didn't squirm away this time. "You snore by the way."

"You fart, hence why I hate you," she replied and brought the coffee to her lips. After the warmth traveled down her chest she winked at him. "All that eating healthy, looks good on the outside, though."

"I just asked them to put lettuce and tomato on my burger. It's good."

"The point of a burger is to clog your pretty little heart with melted cheese and bacon," she said, poking him on his bare chest. "What was so urgent this morning?"

"Karen always gets a call from her mom on election day, I just figured, she wasn't going to get one today and I pinch hit."

"Mary Beth's mom disowned her for a long time. My mom never would. She depends on me too much I guess."

"Kind of a who's the real mother deal?"

"Most times, I think I became more mature than her around age ten, but that may be giving her too much credit."

"You hungry?"

"Not too bad, you didn't really work me out last night."

"I don't plan on it any time soon," Ash stated. "You think you can stand being around me with your clothes on?"

"You can recork the bottle, but the bubbles have all fizzed."

"Trust me, I know how to shake it just right to make it explode again," he whispered in her ear, and then nipped her earlobe. A shot headed south and she had to agree.

When his hand went to her stomach it clenched hoping for more. Praying for it. Damn, she was ready to strip him down right now and take him by force. His lips trailed down her neck to the crook, so lightly she felt lost in the dream of his touch. Her hand ran through his hair to cradle his head and give his lips full contact. Their bodies crashed against each other and her leg locked around his.

"Thank you," she moaned when his hardness rubbed against her center. Sweet tease for the moment, but her body ached for him in a way that few things could satisfy.

His lips crushed against hers and when his tongue stroked into her mouth her knees gave out. Clutching him with all her might, she clung to his biceps. As if she were as light as a pillow, he lifted her so she was sitting on the counter. Wedged between her legs, he continued to kiss her with vigor. She pulled up on his shirt and tossed it to the floor. Their embrace broken for a moment, she could open her eyes and take in his well sculpted chest. Her fingers trailed down from his pecs to his abs, and then tugged on his shorts.

"Shaken, but not stirred," he said, cupping her cheeks and kissing her lightly.

He reached for an apple and walked away with a loud snap as he bit.

"Are you freaking kidding me?" she called after him, afraid to hop down and find no strength left in her body. "If this is what a relationship is, I want none of it."

"Lie again," he called from the bedroom.

"Why would I want to be with a man who leaves me on the edge?"

He poked his head around the corner. With smiling eyes, he smirked.

"Because I took you there."

Chapter Five

"No one is so brave that he is not disturbed by something unexpected."
—Julius Caesar

Mandy answered the door, and Ashton couldn't help smiling at her disheveled hair and tight cami. He'd spent the last week texting and teasing Mandy in ways he didn't know were in him. Now was the test. Had a week away made her want him more?

"It's morning," she grumbled at him.

"I know seeing me in the light of day isn't your favorite thing, but we need to talk."

"Why?" she groaned as she leaned on the door for support.

"Humor me." Ash smiled, cradled her cheek, and kissed her forehead. "I've been thinking."

"And that involves me why?" she asked, padding her way to the kitchen.

"You might be interested in a few things," he replied and kissed her shoulder as she removed a box of fruity-o's from the cabinet.

"I doubt it. The last time I saw you in the light of day I was annoyed."

"You mean in the morning after you woke up in my arms?"

"Yes, between that and the ridiculous idea we should be…what, a couple?"

Mandy poured a bowl of cereal, filled it with milk, and then plopped on her barstool to eat at the counter. Ash marveled at the way her lips surrounded the spoon. Hiking her leg up, she rested her foot on the barstool so one knee was bent and the other leg dangling.

Ash opened a drawer and pulled out another spoon to get his own mouthful of sweetness. She glared at him, and then pulled the bowl tightly to her chest.

"Mine."

"We need to talk about what's going on with the two of us."

"You came over, slept..." She drew out the word as if it were a foreign concept. "Played a little slap and tickle. Then tried to kiss me goodbye before taking off for..." Her spoon spun in the air as she counted the time. "Pretty much a week."

"I called."

"Ah, you interrupted me during important moments in my life."

"Living La Vita Luciano?"

"He had an audition," she balked. "Do you know how many years it's been since he's been in a movie?"

"I think I was five."

"Exactly. He's on a comeback and I needed to see all the training he went through."

"For your next audition?" Ash teased then attempted to get another spoonful, only to have Mandy turn and walk to the couch still holding the bowl to her chest for dear life. She moved a huge pillow over to the side and sat cross legged on the couch as she took another bite.

"You're a child."

"No, a child wouldn't have more than one bowl or additional cereal."

"I don't want a whole bowl," Ash whined.

"I feel like a broken record when you come over," she said as she settled on the couch and wrapped a blanket around her shoulders.

"How is that?"

"Because I don't understand why you are here and you never tell me."

"I want a relationship with you, Amanda. I thought I made that clear."

She looked down into the bowl of fruity-o's and stirred the cereal before finally responding.

"I don't do monogamy."

"Why not? Too much like your dad?"

The glare he got sent a chill from the top of his head down his spine.

"Sorry, low blow."

"My father's a serial monogamist, thank you very much. He just doesn't like ending relationships before their time."

"And their time is?"

"When the women stop fucking him, I assume." She turned her head down and ate a few spoonfuls.

"So that's it, we just see each other around the girls' wedding?"

"I see no reason to do anything else."

Ash crossed his leg at the knee and stared at Mandy. She wouldn't look at him. Instead she would eat, and then look out the window or behind him to the door to her bedroom.

"Unless you want to help me move," she suggested.

"Why are you moving?" he asked, placing both feet on the ground and leaning his elbows on his knees.

"Because Sarah's moving in with Karen, so I need to find a new place. Preferably with four walls, a roof, and a bathroom."

"How about a door to get in?"

"That would be helpful."

"Why can't you stay here?"

"There are two rooms and I don't do roommates. Sarah was an exception."

"How soon do you need to be out?"

"I don't know," she said, shrugging her shoulders. "Sarah hasn't told me when they plan on moving in together."

"Karen hasn't said a word either. Maybe they're waiting until after the election or after they get married," he suggested. "It might be a while."

"Yeah, well, even though you and the Rep aren't a joint package, I'd rather move before getting kicked out. So, we settled? You leaving?"

Ash clucked his tongue a few times and Mandy once again turned her head to the window. A creek sounded behind him and he turned to see a woman tip toeing out of Mandy's room wearing a pair of shorts and a camisole. Her hair was in much the same state as Mandy's.

"Sorry," she apologized as she cut to the bathroom. "I know you said to stay put, but I had to pee."

He swiveled his head back to Mandy. "You picked up a woman."

"Looks that way, doesn't it?" she smirked. "Too bad you weren't with me. It could have been a whole lot of fun."

A sink ran, and then turned off. The woman reappeared, and Ash wished Mandy hadn't planted that idea in his mind. The stranger held her hand out to him.

"I'm Lana, you must be Mandy's brother." She smiled, and he shook her hand. He glanced back at Mandy to find her covering her lips with her hand to hide a smile. "Sorry I'm such a mess."

"I would expect nothing less," he replied. "Well, sis, I better go, you know how the kids get when they aren't supervised."

"Let them out of your sight for a moment and all hell breaks loose," Mandy replied and waved at him with her spoon.

He was starting to realize maybe he didn't have enough energy to even begin setting up a relationship with Mandy, regardless of the feelings telling him she could be the one for him. Maybe her issues were too big. He was five years older than her. Helping a woman grow up wasn't his idea of kicks and giggles.

Too bad, Mandy was all kinds of kicks and giggles.

~ * ~

With a click, the front door closed and Mandy set her bowl down. Tightening the blanket around her shoulders, she gave a half smile to Lana.

"Your brother is hot, too bad he's got kids." She looked over her shoulder. "He looks familiar."

"Just one of those faces. I'm sure it was a windblown guy in a window in the mall or something."

"Probably." She pulled out her ponytail holder so her blonde hair cascaded to her shoulders. "Thanks again for letting me crash here last night. I can't believe I'm not hung over."

"I did all but start an IV on you. You better not have a headache."

"I don't, but what about you? That couch couldn't have been comfy."

"I only fell on the floor twice," she teased. "Half the time I don't make it to my bed lately. Especially since my roommate's been at her girlfriend's so much."

"Okay. Hey are those fruity-o's?"

"Yeah, my niece and nephew spent the night on Thursday and my job is to give them what they can't have. Stinkin' kids wanted oatmeal. What three-year-old wants oatmeal?"

Mandy got ready for the day, which consisted of the only real reality TV she lived for—NFL football. Talk about drama and bullshit. Between the trades, bad calls, and coaches you can't get any better than a Sunday spent watching games. She drove Lana to the bar to pick up her car while listening to the local sports talk. They were discussing some of the players set to be out for the Vikings games this week.

"It's the politics around the trade I don't like," a call in guest said, and Mandy's mind wandered to real politics.

More, a politician, if that's what Ash really was. Although she'd get to spend the Vikings game with Charlie and Claire, the next six hours of football she'd be by herself. Why hadn't she tried to sleep with Lana last night? She'd been more than willing. Then again, why hadn't she seized the opportunity to mix it up with Ash and her this morning?

What the hell were his motives with her? Turning her on…leaving her hanging…calling her like…a shiver shot through her body from her spine down to her toes, which curled. Her phone had a light blinking from a text message and she swiped at the screen. It was from last night, one of Ashton's attempts at flirting.

Maybe…after the kids went home she'd respond to it. If nothing else, he passed the time and it was obvious she was picking up random strangers this week. Why? She didn't know. But there were worse habits to break.

On her way back home, she stopped by for supplies. She wasn't sure why this week seemed different as she grabbed chips, pop, and hot dogs. The small part of her that knew she'd be picking up Claire and Charlie told her to pick up a fruit tray, so she succumbed. But when she turned into the produce section she caught sight of Ashton. Well, his ass anyway. He did have a nice one when he wore the right jeans. The ass called to her and she tried to stop herself from staring. As if he felt the gawking, he turned sharply and her eyes shot up, catching his.

A confused look crossed his face, and then he returned to picking out flavors of bagged salad. He'd seen her for sure. Those baby blues had made enough contact with hers that she was flushed and had even smiled…yes, she was sure she'd smiled. Crossing the distance between them, she rammed her shopping cart into his tight buttocks.

"I've had the best and worst week of my life," he said without turning. "Guess what part you were in?"

"The adorably cute part."

"An hour ago, you were telling me to leave so you could go back to fucking some random woman."

"Lana," she corrected. "and just so you know—"

"That's right, Lana," he said and finally turned. "I got off a plane and came straight to you. Can you think why that would be?"

"Sadomasochism."

"Are you bi-polar?"

"The theory has been batted about more than once, but sadly no."

"How can I help you?" Ash asked as he snatched a cucumber from the pile, only to have Mandy's eyebrow crook up.

"Never wake me before ten on a weekend without good reason."

"I wanted to see you. That seemed good enough for me."

"Not I." She sighed and reached for a fruit tray. "But, I've been thinking about your sick desire to see me on more than one occasion."

"I've been cured of that," he replied. "Got my cooties shot and everything."

"With both X's? Because if you don't do both X's it doesn't count."

"It was stupid of me to ask," he said, tossing the bag salad into his basket. "You are bi-polar."

"Am not, or am…let me ask Suzie Q."

Ash crossed his arms and glared at her. For the first time in recent memory she was ashamed.

"Um, you know, my other personality…"

"Suzie Q," he grumbled and stalked off. "There isn't a version of you that I could ever see being named Suzie."

"She's the sweet side of me." Mandy pushed and double timed it to keep up with Ash. "The kindergarten teacher and all."

"So, not the one who slept with Lana last night."

"No one slept with Lana."

"Right," he chuckled and tossed something into his hand held basket.

"I'm serious," she replied and cut her basket to stop his movement. "She slept in my bed, I slept on the couch."

Ash turned his head and his eyes twitched as if he were replaying the morning's events. His hand went up and his tongue touched his top lip. Mandy sucked in her breath and tried to remember why she was even doing all this. He ignored her for a moment and like a damned child she closed the distance between them until they were nearly touching.

"Ashton, there was a pillow on the couch. I'm not gonna bang someone and then crash on the couch."

"Oh yeah…you're right," he said. "Then why did you tell her not to come out?"

"Because if she saw you she'd probably try to sleep with you."

He smiled. "You were jealous?"

"No. I just didn't feel like getting kicked out of my own apartment once again so someone else can have sex."

"You were jealous," he teased again, and Mandy took off toward the checkout. "Admit it, you don't want me to sleep with anyone else."

"I don't care who you sleep with. In fact, I encourage the behavior."

"Do you now? Hmm…I don't buy it." He placed his basket on the belt first. "I think right now you're dying to take me home and find out what happened in DC."

"Just goes to show what you know. I happen to be picking up a guy and girl and spending the day with them…alone in my apartment."

"Claire and Charlie?" he asked and placed the juice boxes from her cart onto the belt.

"It's NFL Sunday. You have about five minutes to get out of my way so I can get to them and back to my favorite day of the week."

"Really?"

"Yes, I don't lie to you. You assume shit, but I don't lie. You even pointed that out."

"You're right. I did." He turned to the cashier. "Ten bucks if you can get my basket and hers rung through in the next two minutes."

The cashier looked at him strangely, and then scanned the items faster than Ash could get them out of her basket. With a swipe of his card already in place he made sure to ask for ten dollars cash back and proceeded to quickly pack the items in bags.

As they both walked to their cars Mandy still didn't know what happened.

"Give me your apartment key," he ordered. "I'll get all the groceries put away and have the pregame going before you even get home."

"I didn't say I was watching it with you."

"Why not? I'm amazing."

"Be that as it may, little kids have big mouths."

"True, I'll think up a story if they talk."

"Right," she scoffed. He placed his hand on her keys.

"I get paid to convince people."

"Kids are different."

"You mean the ones who aren't scared of a man breaking into their house, eating their cookies, and leaving gifts?"

She almost let slip a giggle. "That's different, they don't see him."

"I'm going to ask you to do the most difficult thing you've ever been asked before in your life."

"You have no clue how flexible I can be," Mandy replied with raised eyebrows.

Ash removed the half of her keys with the apartment key on it.

"Trust me."

~ * ~

After loading the dishwasher and folding the quilt Mandy had slept with on the couch, Ashton surveyed the apartment. Everything finally looked in order so he flipped on the TV. Water boiled on the stove and he placed the hotdogs in the water. On the table, he set the fruit and chips.

"Okay, so remember Auntie Sarah's friend Ashton?" Mandy said as she entered the apartment. "He played catcher because mommy was sick?"

"I doos," the spritely voice of Claire replied. "Daddy can't catch."

Ash peered around the corner, and Charlie curled against Mandy's leg. She lightly petted his tight fade. His dark mahogany eyes, surrounded by thick, black lashes, were curious, but cautious.

"Charlie, right?" Ashton asked. Charlie ducked behind Mandy so all Ashton could see were his hands wrapped around her waist.

"I's Claire." Claire skipped to the kitchen. "Charlie's a scaredy-cat."

"He's just a bit shy until he gets to know you," Mandy corrected as Claire pulled herself up on a chair, and then looked up at Ash.

"Mama cuts 'dem for us."

"I'm sorry, I hadn't gotten that far," Ash apologized and proceeded to cut up the hotdog into bite sized pieces.

"You hungry, Charlie?" Mandy asked as she led him to the table. He shook his head no. "I bet you are, just a bit."

Charlie stayed glued to Mandy's hip. She reached down and flipped him upside down and then back up again until he came to rest straddling her hip. He giggled and buried his face into her neck. Ash took the cue and sat down with Claire as she explained about her pretties. Who knew a little girl could talk so much about a pair of tights? Soon they were all eating as the pregame came on. Mandy looked up at him when Claire said something funny and Charlie laughed.

"Who here likes football?" he asked.

"I like the cracks," Claire howled as she hopped off the chair and took her plate to the sink. Ash looked at Mandy and pointed to the action as if someone under the age of twelve couldn't perform it.

"Told you I didn't teach kindergarten." She smirked as Charlie did the same thing.

"So, what are the cracks exactly?" Ash asked as they finished clearing and moved to the couch.

"You know, silly. When they hug."

"Tackles?" Ash asked. "You like the tackles."

"I lubs a good hug," Claire exclaimed and jumped on Ash. She almost knocked the wind out of him and crushed his manhood. Some hug.

Charlie wasn't as enthusiastic as Claire when he crawled on the chair to sit with Mandy.

"Which game are we watching first?" Ash asked as he pulled up the screen with the two noon offerings.

"Thomas Twins, who do we watch with Auntie Mandy?"

"Da Vikings," the two called and both clapped their hands.

Claire then jumped down and took off to Mandy's room and retrieved a plastic helmet with horns.

"I should have known," he said and made sure they were on the right channel.

Claire wasn't kidding around about loving the cracks, but both she and Charlie did have the attention span of any other three and a half year old. Mandy handled them beautifully as they put puzzles together and worked on math problems.

"That is a big problem," Ash said as he looked at the piece of paper Charlie was working on.

"Auntie Mand is helping me learn my takeaways," Charlie said softly as he worked with large graph paper to keep his numbers in line. "It's not that big if you takes one box at a time."

"I guess not," Ash said as Charlie subtracted twenty-five thousand three hundred and sixteen from fourteen thousand two hundred and two. "Charlie, you know Auntie Mand really well don't you?"

"She's my auntie," he said, smiled and wrote four on his paper, then moved on to the next one box.

"Do you think Auntie Mand needs a boyfriend?"

"Nope," he said as he drew a line for the number one.

"Why not?" Ash asked. He'd never interrogated a preschooler, but love made people do crazy things.

"She's already gots one."

Ash looked into the kitchen where Claire was kneeling on the counter with Mandy standing behind her. They were discussing something as they dug through the cabinet.

"Who?"

"Me, we's getting' married."

"You are?" Ash smiled as Charlie wrote another one.

"Yep."

"Guess I don't have a chance then."

"You can bes her boyfriend too, but I gets to marry her."

64

"You'd share?"

"Why not?" he asked and shrugged his shoulders with his palms up.

"But I can't marry her?"

"No."

"Is he trying to marry your sister?" Mandy teased from the kitchen.

"Yeah," Claire cheered. Mandy scrunched her nose at her.

"No," Charlie replied simply. "You."

Mandy stood still and stared at Ash who leaned back and crossed his legs at the knee.

"Don't look so scared," Ash smirked. "Charlie laid out all the rules. I can date you, but he gets to marry you."

Mandy's lips pursed, and then she returned to dealing with Claire. Ash resumed his awe of Charlie's math skills.

"You sure you're only three?" he asked.

"I's got a burfday soon."

Claire helped Mandy measure out water for the muffin mix she promised them. She clapped as Mandy turned on the mixer. The amazing part is somehow Mandy didn't miss a play on the TV even while helping the kids. With muffins cooking, they cleaned up and soon all of them were eating warm blueberry muffins and high fiving a touchdown.

The knock at the door made Mandy jump.

"Okay double trouble, go get your bags," Mandy ordered.

Ash realized he hadn't given the kids a cover story. He'd been trying to win them over, only to be won over himself.

"What are we going to have them say?" he asked.

"They always give a Readers Digest version of hanging with Auntie Mandy."

Mandy opened the door and Gabbie came in. He could hear them on the other side of the wall talking as he hung out in the kitchen by the fridge.

"Thank you so much, we could've never gotten the things we needed with them."

"Tell me about it," Mandy said as she fell against the wall. "Seriously I don't know how you do it. They are so much trouble."

"Are not," Claire protested.

"Well, maybe not you, but Charlie?" Mandy teased. "Speaking of which, Charlie go grab your work to show mama."

"You made them do school work?" Gabbie asked.

"They are Montessori kids. You don't make them do anything, they choose."

Ashton covered his mouth as he laughed a bit at that. Charlie came over to him and he thought their cover was blown as he tugged on Ash's shirt then held his hand out to shake Ashton's. Ash gave his patented politician shake with two hands. Charlie then pulled him out into the open, but Mandy, the observant, had her back to the two of them. Gabbie's husband, Case, on the other hand was standing in the doorway and looked between Ash and Mandy. He shook his head, but seemed content to stay silent.

"About Charlie," Mandy began. "He's really worried about you."

"What?" Gabbie asked as she helped Claire tie her shoe. "Why?"

The why is where he got caught. She'd looked up at Mandy only to see him on the other side holding her son's hand. Case's mahogany eyes, a Thomas sibling trait, looked down at the floor as he ran his hand over his goatee.

"Well, because you've been sick in the morning he feels bad because he can't help you," Mandy explained, but Gabbie was still staring straight at Ashton with her gray eyes. "You need to tell them. I think it's time, especially since, you know…"

Gabbie still hadn't broken eye contact with Ashton. "You're teaching them s-e-x ED?"

"Please, five minutes around you and—" Mandy turned and bit her top lip. "Crap sticks."

"At least we don't need the swear jar today." Gabbie stood and crossed her arms. "Wanna tell me something?"

"Hey, look at that, Claire, the Vikings got a sack," Case said as he scooped her up and slapped Ash's shoulder. Ash instantly understood this as being Pure Man Talk for, *Let us extricate ourselves from this situation post haste.*

"Yeah, a crack," she called as the four of them went to the couch. Mandy and Gabbie retired to the bedroom. Ash assumed to avoid a crack in real time.

"So, how long has she been in love with you?" Case asked.

"Ah, um…" Ashton stumbled nervously, then leaned his elbows on his knees. "Other way around," he admitted. "I can barely get her to be around me."

"Yep, must be love." Case laughed. "Want me to call her out on it?"

Chapter Six

"A confession has to be part of your new life."
—Ludwig Wittgenstein

"Anything you'd like to say?" Gabbie asked when they got in Mandy's room and closed the door.

"Not really."

"Right, because you never apologize for your behavior, I forgot."

"What behavior should I be apologizing for?" Mandy asked.

"You can't honestly tell me that you had a guy in the house all this time and didn't do anything."

"Yes, I can." Mandy huffed as she crossed her arms. "Contrary to popular belief I can just have a friend."

"Please, with the walking sex god out there."

"Case?" she laughed. "He couldn't make it out of the friend zone with me."

"Very funny. Ash is...he's..."

"What is he?" she asked. "Karen's best friend. A stand-up guy. The man who drives me nuts when he's around."

"You love him."

"The hell I do," Mandy howled.

"Oh, my God." Gabbie laughed and covered her mouth. "You're in love."

"I'm barely lustful with his Cro-Magnon ass." Mandy began pacing around the room. "That's what I love. His ass. It's...you tell anyone and I'll..."

"You're in love."

68

"It's your fault."

"Why? Because I wouldn't marry you?"

"No," Mandy scoffed as she finally stopped moving. "You and Mary Beth and Sarah. You're all falling in love and that shit is catching. I was happy before. It's more Sarah's fault, dropping sex on a stick out there in my living room like I wouldn't mind."

It was at this point Mandy lost her mind. Looking back years later, she'd come to realize it was the tipping point that sent her into Ash's arms. Still flailing her arms, she continued her rant about the disgust of love in all its forms. The betrayal of her friends for bringing that shit into her life.

"You done?" Gabbie asked, looking at her phone for the time. "How about I'll keep this little secret for you if you let me be there when you run off to Vegas with him."

"Seems fair," Mandy agreed, knowing there was no way in hell she'd be going anywhere with Ashton Gilmore.

"We good?" Case asked as they both emerged from the bedroom.

"Yep, time to get home and start supper."

"I'm not hungry, mama," Claire said. "I had lots of cake."

"Blueberry muffins," Mandy said with her hands up in the air to avoid mama rage. "And it was only one and a half."

Gabbie butted in, "Ashton, good to see you again, but just know next year I won't need a back up."

"I wouldn't think of taking your spot on the team." He smiled and stood up. Goodbyes were cordial and, thankfully, brief.

Finally alone in the apartment, Mandy rested on the arm of her couch and looked at Ash.

"Here's the deal," she started. "The whole…relationship thing, I don't do, and I don't understand why you're pressuring me."

Ashton sighed and ran his fingers through his sandy blond hair.

"I apologize. I didn't realize I was pressuring you." Ash stood and began to walk to the door.

"Wait," Mandy called. The word caught in her throat. It felt strange.

"I like you. A lot. I can't be the first man…person…whatever that's wanted to spend more than five minutes with you."

"People that stay around me do so for a reason."

"That they like you?" Ash suggested as he placed both hands on the counter, causing his forearms to flex. Mandy tried to focus on the human and not the body in front of her.

His face contorted as if she'd confused him. Probably matching her face.

"I'm the body," she said as she stood and ran her hands along her sides. "The party girl on the crazy scale that men like to fuck and hang out with just to say they had a girl as hot as me."

Ash sucked his lips to stifle his smile.

"I know what I have going for me. One thing. Just one."

"You're the dumbest smart person I've ever met." Ash laughed. "And probably have the lowest self-esteem of any human on the planet."

"I'm fucking amazing," Mandy snapped. She'd never believed those words she'd quoted for years.

"The fucked up thing is, Mandy, you are. You just don't see it. Sadly, if anyone wants to show you, all you do is shove them away." Ash crossed the room and pulled her into his arms. "Right now, if I told you how I really feel about you you'd probably end up kneeing me in the crotch and forcing me out of the building."

Her breath caught as the warmth of his body enveloped her. Held tightly against him, she wanted to pull away, needed too. Instead of feeling protective, the strong arms were claustrophobic and all consuming. She couldn't find herself. Instead she was a part of something…someone. Suddenly fire burned in her lungs, scorching in a way she couldn't breathe. With shallow gasps her chest tightened and she feared what would happen if she didn't get away.

"I love you, Amanda…I didn't want to. Trust me, the last thing I need is to fall in love with a woman incapable of any emotion that isn't flight mode."

"Stop it." She shoved against his chest, but he didn't budge, not an inch, and that was when Mandy realized she barely pushed. She didn't want to push. Ash was right—her flight instinct consumed her most days. Only with her friends did she stay, but they were pairing off. Although they'd always be there for her, she would be even more of an outsider.

Ash brushed back her hair and cradled her face in his hands. Kissing her lips, he didn't push…or press hard. Instead he was lightly brushing his lips across hers. No longer held in his arms, she found herself wrapping her arms around him and clinging to his back. When he released her from his sweet caress, his hands went down her back and rested on her hips.

"Right now, Ash, I need you," she confessed.

"I'm here for you, Mandy. I'm not going anywhere."

"You don't get it. I need you, I don't want you…well, I want you, but need is where I'm at."

He stepped back and her hands glided around his sinewy back. The cuts of his muscles had every inch of her quivering.

"I'm at want. My options are open and it's ridiculous how many women want to console me in my time of need. But I want to be with you. You consume my thoughts."

A buzzing surged through her body as he stroked her hair and nipped at her ear. Her lips quivered when his neck brushed against them and he seemed content to take it no further. Her core was heavy and aching as the need to be with him built. Unlike before in her life when anyone would do, now there was only one person in the world who could satisfy her.

"Ash," she panted as her fingers curled in the belt loops of his pants. "You have me. Now please for the love of all that is holy, do something with me."

He scooped her up in his arms and her head lolled to his chest. She wanted to praise him because she was unsure her legs would have held her much longer. The fresh scent of his cologne crept into her lungs, increasing her desire. Wetness pooled between her legs as a moan escaped her lips. He laid her out on the bed and she closed her eyes and rolled her head back. With a fury, she unfastened her pants, only to have his hands cover hers as his body engulfed hers.

"You need me, I want you…" he growled into her ear. "Let me show you the difference."

His lips brushed against hers and hungrily she attacked him, only to have him back away. His cool blue eyes were swimming with lust, and she knew they were matched in sexual aching. A hard shaft pressed between her thighs, adding to the slickness that begged to be used.

When cold chills ran over her, she finally opened her eyes to see Ashton standing at the edge of the bed. The sound of his zipper echoed in her room and she realized she'd stopped breathing. It wasn't until she heard the plop of his pants hitting the floor that she found air again. With a sharp inhale, she eyed his cock, thick with desire as a small pearl of cum rested at the tip. Pushing up on her elbows, she widened her legs.

"Did I say you could move?" he asked as he pulled off his shirt and tossed it to the floor.

She salivated at the sight of his naked form. He was slightly tanned with a craggy hardness that she needed pressed against her body.

"I said lay down," he commanded. She fell back on her pillow. With three big tugs, her pants were off and he climbed over her like a panther. Every muscle bulged and stretched until he was pressed between her legs.

Her nipples perked against her bra, the sting of the fabric burned her sensitive flesh and she reached to pull Ash. He caught her halfway and pinned her hands above her head. Then with his other hand he wasted no time in removing her shirt and bra. His lips surrounded her nipple as his tongue swirled around the tip and started tugging on it a bit.

"Ash, please, I need you," she gasped, unsure why she was still wearing her panties.

"Wants usually come with delayed gratification," he whispered as he licked along her neck and sucked on her earlobe. "Big purchases and all."

"I'm not a purchase."

"Fine," he sighed. "That vacation you want to go on, but don't necessarily need."

He flipped her over and Mandy buried her head in her pillow as he once again disappeared from her body. This time his lips found the back of her knee and began the trek to her ass. Kisses and licks led by the light brushing of his nose against her skin let her know his next step. Her fingers bunched her sheets as heat crashed against chills on her skin. The tease was agonizing to her. She swore her heartbeat pounded against every inch of her. When she finally felt Ash nibbling on her ass cheek she groaned and arched her butt up in the air. His long fingers slid under her panties, then removed them in a way that caused his hands to have

72

contact with her and nothing else.

The drawer next to her bed swished as it opened and she clenched, knowing he'd finally retrieved a condom. Soon he'd be filling her to his hilt and the anguish would be over. She could be satisfied. Ash placed two kisses on the dimples at the base of her back, and then used his thumbs to spread out the bottom of her butt. The rest of his hands wrapped around her hips.

She was so wet he didn't need to guide his shaft into her. Instead he teased the outside of her up and down a few times until he thrust hard and filled her to capacity. She spasmed around him, and when he pulled back to begin his rhythm, she couldn't believe she was already cumming all around his thick hardness. Quicker than she thought possible, but he'd just begun. His strokes were slow at first, and torturous. Her breasts ached from the desire weighing them down. They burned as he continued to pump. His strong hands clutched her hips.

When his pace quickened, she came again, harder, tightening around him, but instead of slowing him down he increased with a howl. Proclaiming her pussy the best he'd ever known. How her ass was perfection. She bit the pillow in front of her as he brought her to ecstasy and refused to let her come back down. Her hands reached for anything to ground her, but she might as well have been on a slick surface. Ash delivered, hard and fast as he smashed deep inside her. When his stroke turned regular and fast she knew he was close and right as he came, she clenched every muscle in her body. She felt him still twitching inside her as they both collapsed onto the bed without losing their connection.

~ * ~

Ash kept Mandy flush to his body as her skin, slick with a mist of sweat, caused them to stick together in the most pleasurable of ways. Even as he was softening inside her, he didn't want to pull out, but he had no choice. As they spooned he caressed her shoulder, and then reached behind him to pull the blanket around the two of them. The tight burrito-like wrapping they were in was something Mandy fought normally. Today she was pressing against him and pulling his arm tightly to her body.

He kissed her shoulder and prepared to fall into a wonderful Sunday afternoon nap. Mandy snuggled slightly against him as she too was falling into sleep in the warm cocoon. The front door creaked open.

"Mandy," Sarah called. Both lovers stiffened.

A set of keys landed on the counter, and Mandy shot from his arms.

"Stay here," she whispered, snatching her cami and throwing it over her head. "And quiet."

"Gabbie knows about us."

"And she's sworn to secrecy."

"Are any of you girls really secret?"

Mandy glared at him while pulling on her sweatpants and heading out the door.

"Really?" he heard Sarah chastise Mandy when she emerged. "It's four o'clock on a Sunday."

"And the Vikings won, you know how that gets me going."

"A strong breeze gets you going." Sarah sighed.

"Depends on the direction," Mandy replied. "Why are you here?"

"Just grabbing some stuff. I would have called Ash, but I know how you feel about him."

Ash perked up at the change of conversation as he too began retrieving his clothes.

"I just said it was rude to have a stranger show up in my house."

"Ash isn't strange," Sarah said. "You'd be lucky to have a guy as nice as him date you."

"If you try to set us up I'll cut you in your sleep."

"And you wonder why I sleep at Karen's."

"I figured it was because she has the better strap on."

"Why must everything you say be crude?"

"I have a twelve-year-old boy trapped inside me," Mandy replied. "Don't tell child protection. He's my dirty little secret."

"Whatever." Sarah's voice became solemn. "I worry about you Mand. Are you sure you're okay with me spending so much time with Karen?"

"I wouldn't expect anything less. You know me, I love my alone time. Plus someone told my mom where I live, so she tends to pop up randomly."

"What's the latest?"

"I don't know or care. Any woman who thinks the wife of the man she's committing adultery with is using her cancer to keep him needs to be beaten."

Sarah let out another sigh. Ash had a feeling by the extended silence that Sarah was hugging Mandy.

"I feel sorry for the man you fall in love with."

"Why?" Mandy chuckled.

"Because when you finally open up your heart it's going to be all consuming. If he's not ready…hey, what does it matter? It will be years, right?"

"Decades at least. I need to get my funky on."

"Just not so much with yourself, okay," Sarah suggested. Ash heard the keys being picked up.

When the door closed, he poked his head out of the bedroom. He saw Mandy stretched on the couch flipping off the Packers who'd scored on the Lions.

"It safe?" he asked.

"Yep, so you leaving?"

"I didn't want to."

"Good," Mandy turned and looked at him with longing in her eyes. "How much did you hear?"

"You masturbate when the Vikings win?" he teased.

"They shouldn't be the only ones to score."

"Is it on a one to one ratio? You know, one touchdown a go? Or do field goals count?"

"Depends on the distance." Mandy smiled. "That wasn't what I was wondering."

"I'm not scared about you loving me too much."

"I hate you, that would never be an option."

"It's a thin line."

"Yes, but usually you hate the ones you once loved."

"Lucky for me, you hate me." Ash grinned and crawled on top of Mandy, who opened her legs to give him a place to settle into.

"Yeah, but the Pack scored, which is worse than a cold shower."

"Or make up sex."

"Never tried that."

"I foresee us fighting quite a bit, so I'm sure we'll be having lots of it." His hand snuck under her cami and wound its way to her breast. Fitting nicely in his palm he swore the first time he saw them they were fake. Round and perfectly perked, but no. They were a hundred percent real and tasted of peaches. "Mandy, will you be my girlfriend?"

"I don't do labels."

"Mandy, will you stop sleeping with other people and only sleep with me?"

"I don't know," Mandy said. "You think you can handle my needs?"

"Are you challenging my manhood again?"

"Is there any manhood to challenge?" She smirked and pressed his hardness against her covered core. As he claimed her lips he knew she'd be his. She was falling further into him and he just needed to make sure he never let her slip through his fingers.

Chapter Seven

"Love and pain become one in the same in the eyes of a wounded child."
—Pat Benatar

For the next two months, Ashton and Mandy made time for each other while he worked on both Karen's campaign and issues with the RNC as a whole. Mandy tried not to share her annoyance about Karen passive aggressively pointing out Ash's constant absence as an issue to her campaign.

She wanted to like Karen, if for no other reason than to support Sarah. But it was hard when Ash's loyalty never wavered. It wasn't his employment with her that made her requests higher than those in DC. He loved her, deeply. Mandy wondered from time to time, when the room was quiet and no one was looking, if he could someday love anybody else that way. Not her, of course, but someone.

That November, as she sat in the room filled with Karen's staff members, she could see Ash's focus on the numbers. He didn't want her to lose, but truly he had no place anymore if she did. The local state house didn't need him in an advisory role because coming out had pretty much decided the trajectory of her political future. She had vigor and surety that one would expect from a politician. No longer doubting herself, she knew what and who she was.

Ash's jaw twitched as the numbers flipped for the third time in a row. Each cycle of results changed the one in the lead. His hand flipped because his phone hadn't left his palm in an hour. She wanted to rub his shoulders and tell him it would work out the way it should. The last thing she expected at eighteen was to own her own business, but now she couldn't imagine her life without Growing Strong Montessori.

The strangest part was that although they'd slipped a few times, for the first time in her life she had a relationship. Where talking and laughing occurred. They checked in with each other and she knew more about his situation in DC than Karen did. Than most people had known. Time to themselves had become precious and sacred. Not having pressure from her friends to give up "the dish" had made the situation better.

When he ran his fingers through his blond hair, then began rubbing his neck, she was ready to out the two of them. It was time. He needed her right now and when he turned and their eyes caught she placed her hands on the table to get up.

A text vibrated her phone.

O.M.G Mandy your father and I are having another baby.

Mandy gave the only response a sane person would.

"What the fuck?" she snapped, and then looked at Sarah who'd been dozing off on Karen's arm. "My mom is pregnant. I need to go...see Mary Beth before..."

Mandy looked back at Ash who'd stood and walked toward a back door. By the time she got to her car she was in tears and Ash had his arms wrapped around her.

"I hate them. I hate them both. I hate everything."

"I know, baby," he said as he gently stroked her hair while she cried into his chest.

Large sobbing cries shook her whole body.

"It's all your fault," she cried as she shoved him away. "I controlled my feelings. I could keep them in. Then you came along and made me...you made me feel. I shouldn't care that my mother's a dumbass and my father's a fuck up. I hurt, Ash."

He stood a step away appearing blurry, like a painting that had been set out in the rain.

"I don't cry, I don't love, and I sure as hell don't care about anyone or anything."

Pain seared through her chest and she placed her hand there, and then crouched to the ground. Breaths of air became hard to swallow. She became light headed. A hand went to her head and slowly pushed it down until it was between her knees and she fell back on the ground.

Her ass froze from the light snow dropping flurries on the pavement where she sat. Content she was finally able to find purchase with her gasps. Ash's hand then moved to her back and rubbed circles.

"Mary…Beth…will…die…she can't…my mom…"

"Stop until you've fully caught your breath."

"My whole life…they were right."

"Not about you and that's all that matters. And not about your mother."

"She'd been trying to get him," Mandy confessed as her head rose. "He didn't plan this, she did. She was tired of waiting. That woman raised me. What kind of person am I?"

"Stop. You're not her."

"To them I am. I…"

"Ash, they need you," a man said as he poked his head out the door.

"Coming," he replied. "Get in your car, but don't leave. I'm sure it's nothing and I'll be right back."

He helped her to her feet and into her car before abandoning her. As she watched him leave all she could think was how typical this all was. First, he gave her feelings, and then failed to show her how to deal with them. Peeling out, she tore down the road unconcerned for anyone or anything except her newly discovered sister.

~ * ~

"Ash," Sarah said as she came to him. "We're at a meltdown level somewhere below nuclear."

"That's good, nuclear you just have to evacuate until the half life wears off."

"I'm serious, I can't get her calmed down."

Ashton peeked around the corner to see Karen in the back conference room. It seemed to be in one piece. Sarah must be crazy. Then he noticed Karen laying on her back in the middle of the table, silent. That was scary.

"We're going to have to fight." Karen's voice was distant as she mumbled to herself. "The numbers are too close and the lawyers are going to fight. We'll tie up the seat until May."

"I'm not sure it will take that long," Ash said as he sat on the table next to her, but she didn't acknowledge him.

"Should I concede? Yes, there will be other races. But if I back out the RNC won't talk to me ever again. I can't be a Dem, no, not a Dem. Not an Independent. Oh God, I'm going to end up in the Green Party."

"What set her off?" he asked Sarah.

"I don't know. She said we'd have to wait, and then she disappeared. I've tried to talk to her, but nothing." Sarah crawled on the long table too and stroked Karen's hair.

"Here's where you guys are," Howard said as he sauntered in. "We need to respond to Barbara's declaration."

"What declaration?"

"She'd be fighting to make sure every vote counts." Howard's eyebrows knitted together as he scanned the table and came to Karen's prone muttering. "What is she doing?"

"Solving world hunger?" Ashton joked. "Last I knew it was called an aneurism."

"Stop teasing, Ash," Sarah said with concern covering her face. "She's lost."

Why did Karen and Mandy both have to crash at the same time?

"Sarah…" He hesitated sending her out to Mandy. Doing so meant she'd know about the two of them. "Kiss her forehead."

Ash took Karen's hand in his and tried to be as soothing as he could.

"Kare Bear, I need you to focus. Focus on my voice." Ash nodded to Sarah who laid a delicate peck on Karen's forehead. "Kare Bear, we need to bring you back to us."

"It'll never end," she mumbled. "I just wanted a wife and a few kids. Is that so wrong?"

"No, Kare Bear, but I need you to talk to me, not the air. Come on, baby."

Karen began a rant of the crises set to be on the house floor in the next session she'd have to postpone. "The education bill will be delayed. School lunches…Medicaid was supposed to be revamped…all because of lawyers and voting errors. There would be booth errors, strange marks on the form, and bastards…children are going to starve and die! Die, all because of a margin too small to exist. Die!"

"True, Kare Bear, but we need you here with us," Ash said as he kissed the inside of her palm.

Suddenly Karen's eyes twitched as she took in her surroundings, quickly sat up, and grabbed her forehead.

"Praised be his name, father, she is alive." Ash made sure her eyes were completely focused before he backed off. "So…how ya been?"

Karen looked from him to Sarah and back again. The room was silent as everyone waited for a coherent statement.

"Call Barbara's team, the RNC and the election board," she ordered Howard. "We're fighting, but we won't be dirty. I still have an elected office."

"Are you good?" Ash asked as he cupped her cheeks. Her eyes, which he used to be able to decode with a single glance, were now a mystery to him.

"Where's Sarah?"

"I'm right here," Sarah said, and Ash released Karen.

He stepped back and they embraced in a hug. He stood there, awkwardly.

Why was he even here? Sure, he got her to come back to reality, but Sarah could have done that. If nothing else, he'd trained her right. He felt useless being here instead of with Mandy who had to be in full meltdown mode by now.

"We good here?" he asked Howard.

"What's more important than the here and now?" Howard snapped as he stormed out of the room with Ash in lock step behind him. "Seriously, Ash, I know how it feels to be courted by those in power. I know the draw, but sometimes you have to think of the bigger picture."

"What bigger picture is that?"

"Karen is going to go all the way. This bump is going to leapfrog her ahead of those you're on the way to go rescue."

"Howard, you have no idea what you're talking about."

"Let me guess, one of the RNC members called and said to step away now because there's a bigger issue. Bigger candidate," Howard howled. "No one is bigger than Karen at this time."

Ash wasn't sure who he was trying to convince.

"I haven't had a call from the committee."

"Bullshit. I know Vic's been sniffing around. And all those trips you've been taking. You think I haven't noticed?"

"Amazing how Karen hasn't cared."

"Maybe if you would have held your post next to her she wouldn't be breaking down right now."

"Are we tossing blame? Is that where we are? Because, Howard, you kept her trapped until, like an animal, she snapped and bit your hand off. Guess what, yes Vic's been calling me because he saw me as the one who managed her, not you. You may know the way to win, but you can't handle the people. Sorry to say it's not a simulation. You actually have to factor in more than a platform and check off boxes."

"You're such an expert, why don't you just head out to DC and leave us to flounder? Trust me, I can get this under control better than you, sunshine."

"What's going on?" Karen interrupted. "Why is Ash going to DC?"

"Because the RNC called. They want him," Howard tattled.

"But you work for me," Karen said. He could see the stress had brought her to complete exhaustion. "I can't do this without you."

"You don't need me anymore," Ash said. "I'll stay as long as I can, but Karen, you have Sarah."

"Sarah doesn't know politics, she's just a teacher." Karen turned and saw Sarah looking at the floor. "I didn't mean that the way it sounded."

"No, you're right, I'm not a politician."

"Karen, all I did was hold your hand and let you release stress." Ash walked to Sarah and put his arm around her shoulder. "And Sarah does that way better than I do."

"You do more than that," Karen said.

"What, fight with assholes?" Ash asked. "Quit selling Sarah short. The only difference between the two of us is she's not getting paid."

"Then maybe you shouldn't be either," Karen said firmly. "I don't need window dressing. If that's all you are."

"You're firing me?" Ash felt a pang of uncertainty. He'd worked with or for Karen for his entire adult life.

"Sounds like you quit to me."

"Karen," Sarah said as she crossed to her and took her hands in hers. "You're stressed, don't make this decision now."

"Sarah, he made the decision. I'm just helping him confirm his choice."

"You heard her," Howard added. "Go do whatever was more important than this. We have work to do."

"But…" Ash looked at everyone dumbfounded. It was only Sarah who had consoling eyes. The rest of the office held a mix of indignation and embarrassment for overhearing the fight. "Right, guess I can tell Victor I have nothing holding me back now."

"Guess so," Howard said and scratched something on a piece of paper.

~ * ~

Mandy looked at her phone and saw it was close to midnight. Shit. She dialed Mary Beth's number. It took two attempts before she groggily picked up.

"Sarah, tell her congrats," Mary Beth grumbled. "I'm going back to bed."

"It's Mandy, we need to talk."

"Huh?"

"I'm outside your apartment."

Mandy heard shuffling through the door and when it opened Mary Beth was more awake than she sounded a minute ago. Her red hair was sticking out in the back, but her hazel eyes with green speckles were wide awake.

"What happened?" she asked with a panicked tone.

"This will require ice cream."

Mary Beth nodded and went to the kitchen to retrieve the only thing that got the girls through disasters. Pistachio ice cream and chocolate syrup for Mandy. When she went to grab bowls Mandy stopped her.

"Just spoons."

"This is about Dad, isn't it?" Mary Beth replied with her head low.

"Well, since your mother insists on having cancer and not being cured my mother had to do something."

"Jesus, Mary, and Joseph what did they do now?" Mary Beth asked and scooped a spoonful of ice cream out and placed it in her mouth to brace herself.

The girls had become closer than ever since discovering they were sisters. Especially since their mothers and father were acting like some horrible reality show Mandy would normally mock. Instead she was stuck living in the disaster that was Father Dates All. No longer fighting about who did what to whom, they'd both conceded that their mothers were morons and their father was a slut.

"I wanted to be the first to tell you, my mom is pregnant."

Mary Beth choked on her ice cream. She barely managed to swallow as she slapped the counter to help find air. As she gasped she stared at Mandy, but all they could do was shake their heads.

"Would it be wrong to pull them all into a room and smack the shit out of them?"

"Mary Beth, you said a cuss. About damn time."

"How old is your mom? Really? How did she even get pregnant?"

"Well, when a man gets a hard-on he lies and says he loves you so he can empty his sack into your vagina."

Mary Beth gave her patented annoyed glare, and then shoveled five spoonfuls of ice cream in her mouth before she could speak again.

"Is it wrong that I had Luke because I love him, not to keep Nate?" Mary Beth asked. "Aren't children supposed to be had for love, not pawns to keep a man around?"

"I think you were had for love," Mandy said. "I was an accident."

"But your mom wouldn't move on from Dad."

"It took you six years to move on from Nate," Mandy pointed out.

"I just wanted my mom to accept me, and that couldn't happen if I wasn't with Luke's dad." Mary Beth grabbed the carton of ice cream and walked to her couch, where the girls sat with it between them each taking turns eating. "It was stupid, but I was seventeen and didn't know better. Your mom was only eighteen when she got pregnant with you. If she would have met someone like Eli, maybe we wouldn't be in this situation."

"But we are. Another Wallace or Butler will be here soon. Where is your mom with the divorce?"

"Dad's been trying to convince her he wants to stay."

"Sleeping with my mom should convince her."

"I need something else. Anything. Please tell me something good."

Mandy ate more ice cream and curled tighter into herself. Her phone buzzed, but she feared looking at it. What if her mother wanted more from her? She never replied with a *sweet* or a *yeah*. How could she? She wasn't happy to be having another sibling. She was disgusted by her mother's manipulation and scheming. Ever since Mary Beth discovered the truth, Mandy's mother no longer saw the secrecy as a barrier. Kevin had no excuse. The kids were older and it was time to get married. She'd been with him for twenty-five years. With every delay in his divorce her mom had blamed everyone but the man she should.

"Come on, Mandy." Mary Beth prodded Mandy until she came out of her thoughts. "You've been in a good mood lately, something must have happened. Spill."

"I tell you we're about to have a brother or sister and you want gossip?"

"My brain is on overload and I can't wake up Eli to cry on his chest as I scream at the world."

"Then do it to me," Mandy said. "I'm your sister, not just one of your best friends. My job is to back your play and be a sounding board."

"It must be really good." Mary Beth shifted and reached for a throw pillow. "Do you think we're both sex fiends because of our dad?"

"You've been with two guys," Mandy said and laughed. "That a sex fiend does not make."

"Quantity isn't about number of partners," Mary Beth said with an arched eyebrow.

"Sweet Eli? Can he keep up?"

"Very few men can," Mary Beth said with a sigh. "Must be why you don't try to stay with one person. You'd kill them."

Ash had yet to call uncle on her yet, she mused with a slight smile, and then returned to the original question.

"We were both raised by him, I guess. Me not every day, but he did make an effort to make me feel welcome at your house. Even being a sounding board when I was frustrated. I guess he was a dad to me, sort of."

"If we subtract the relationship stuff," Mary Beth began as her hands became overly expressive. "And just look at how he was with the two of us…he is a good dad."

"And it would have been hard if we knew we were sisters growing up."

"You think?"

"I would have understood the tension between our moms, but I never demanded his time. I was happy when I got it, but if I knew he was my dad I would have been hurt most days."

"Because he picked us over you?"

"Yeah."

That revelation hit hard. Mandy floundered for something to say. "So this kid, what do you think he'll do?"

"Will my mom finally leave him you mean?"

Mandy nodded. "I think so. I have a feeling your other sibs are going to be hip to the whole thing soon."

"How does that work? I mean, five red heads, but I'm kind of the stepchild in a way. Who will be the most hated?"

"Hopefully Kevin Wallace will get his comeuppance."

"I doubt it."

Mandy snuggled against Mary Beth and began to cry again. Twice in one day.

Her phone buzzed again. Then again. She finally picked it up and saw multiple texts from Ash checking on her. He wanted to know she was safe and okay. If not he'd come to her. He begged her to respond to him.

With my sister now, but I'll need you tomorrow.

I WANT to help you in any way I can. I'll be at your apartment after work.

She stared at the word want in all caps. Shouldn't it be *need*? It was then she wondered which word was actually stronger. Her mother didn't need her father, but she wanted him. She wanted him in ways that caused her to take steps most would run from. That Mandy would be able to sprint top speed from.

As Mary Beth took on the older sister role and ran her fingers through Mandy's hair to console her, she wasn't sure where her life was going, but Ash would be part of it. Not because she needed him, but because she wanted him to be part of it.

Chapter Eight

"With a new day comes new strength and new thoughts."
—Eleanor Roosevelt

With Mandy in the wind until after work, Ash looked around his condo and wasn't sure what to do. Not waking to an alarm, his body still woke at six. He'd tried to go back to sleep, but it was no good. His first thought was to check on updates on the election, but it still hadn't been called. Both sides tried to play to the electorate.

It'd been a while since he'd had a real day off, so after the gym he headed to his dad's. Carlton Gilmore lived three houses away from Karen Lindstrom's childhood home on Lake Jane. The one time outskirt town now was a fully-fledged suburb with all the honor that bestows upon a person.

Having retired a few years before, Carlton tended to putz around his house during the morning only to venture out in the afternoon for his much needed supplies from whatever he'd found was wrong in the home. Ash's mother had left after he graduated high school and moved to Oregon. They rarely spoke anymore.

"Shouldn't you be working?" his father asked as he came from the garage where he'd been winterizing his boat.

"Karen fired me," Ash replied as he accepted the standard firm handshake from his father.

"I'm sure it was well deserved," he teased.

"Of course."

"I'm assuming you'll be going back to work tomorrow."

"I'm not sure."

His father nodded and they went into his house. The coffee was hours old since his dad had the same alarm setting Ash had, too frickin' early. Tossing out the grounds, Carlton started another pot and they sat at the round kitchen table across from each other.

"Is it because of that girl?"

"Mandy? Yes, no. I had a double melt down last night. For the first time, Karen wasn't my priority."

"Bet she didn't like that."

"I'm not sure she really noticed, but Howard did and thought it was about DC."

"Have you decided about that yet?"

"I have to fly out tomorrow."

"So soon after an uncalled election?"

"It's time to start strategizing for the next one," Ash sighed. "You know with all the shuffling, and it looks like we have a majority right now even with Karen's seat in question."

"Time to take over the world and all."

"You know the presidential election is up next."

His father stretched his long legs out and sat back in his chair. Drumming his fingers on the table at first Ash could see the question forming in his mind. Carlton was a tempered man and made sure important comments were thought out fully before they were made. Ashton had learned to wait for his father's pearls of wisdom, because they were what he reached for in times of struggle.

"Do you…" He reached from his coffee cup and swirled the liquid around before setting the cup down again. "Do you enjoy politics? It seems that you've just been riding Karen's coattails because you didn't want to think about the future."

"I wouldn't be going to DC if I didn't enjoy it."

"Maybe I'm not saying this right. You were a kid running around with a toy fireman's helmet telling everyone you were going to be a fireman."

"Well, I never wanted to be one."

"You know what I mean. Every kid has a dream job when they were younger. I wanted to be a garbage man."

Ash's eyebrows knitted together as he held in a laugh.

"I was five," his dad clarified. "And they used to have really cool hats."

"Right," Ash laughed. "You guys let me be a kid. It's not that I didn't think about different jobs, but they were jobs, not careers. Karen focused enough for the two of us."

"That's my point. Instead of rushing off to another job in the same field, take a few weeks and think about what you want."

Ash shifted in his seat. If he was staying in politics, national was the way to go. He wanted bigger. A different breed of politician lived there. Maybe he'd be a lobbyist or stay a consultant. The sad part was, he didn't really have a political affiliation besides supporting Karen. He could have just as easily been a full blown Communist.

Besides, how could Mandy leave a business she'd built and friends she'd kill for? He didn't think either one of them would survive a long distance deal. He sighed and stared out the window.

"If I step away now, this opportunity will be gone. Right now, they still have me working for Karen. They pay for me to come out there and send a check for my time. I'm not on their payroll."

"Are you going to tell them?"

Ash became distracted by a flash of dark hair bobbing outside the window. "Huh? Tell them what?"

"That you've been fired."

"Come on, we both know Karen's not the firing type. She's just pissy right now."

"Has she ever fired you before?" his dad asked. "I know you two fight like an old married couple, but I don't remember her totally tossing you away."

Ash shrugged off the comment and studied the lake. There, by the docks for her parent's home. Even though it was probably ten degrees out, he saw her sitting on a bench at the end of it. Guess she went back to her security blanket. It was a good thing her parents were still letting her be around them.

"Let me check," Ash said and pushed back from the table. Crossing through the McCarthys' yard, he trotted down the dock. "Hey, Kare Bear."

She turned slowly, and he saw the tears streaking down her cheeks. "Did…d…did I fire you last night?"

"Yep," he replied, stuffing his hands in his pockets.

"But you still came to help me?"

"I was visiting my dad," he confessed and plopped on the bench next to her. They both looked out across the lake with small patches of ice floating on top.

"It'll be at least a month."

"That what Howard said?"

"I meant before we can ice fish."

"Oh," Ash crinkled his nose. "The important things. You going for pneumonia until then?"

Karen pulled her sweater tighter around her shoulders.

"Where's Sarah?"

"Teaching."

"What help did you need, Kare?"

"Um…see," she replied with tears pooling in her eyes. "I don't want to leave Sarah, but I may not get a second chance."

"Bullshit. You're scared."

"Am not, I have a good case. I may just win this one, but I already have an elected office."

"Oh good, they're right on time," Ash said as he pointed over Karen's shoulder until she turned.

"Who?" she asked. There was no one there.

"The people with the cross. I mean, you are a martyr, right?" Ash placed his hands on his chest. "No, no I love you too, I just want to make sure everyone gets a chance to play."

"And you wonder why I fired you."

"Because the truth sucks and I'm the only one unafraid to hold up a mirror."

"Among other things," Karen said as she stood. "What should I do, Ash?"

"Go with your gut. If it says you'll win, then you will."

"That doesn't help with Sarah."

"You'll be getting married soon, it's not really an issue. She's committed to you."

A pang hit Ash as he remembered Mandy ranting at him about having her discover love in all its disgusting reality. Could the two of them ever reach a level of commitment where he'd actually have to consider his future?

"That's what it's about isn't it?" she asked. "Being with someone, not for them."

~ * ~

"All right, Children's House, it's time to pick up or label your work," Mandy told her class as she clasped her hands together.

Some children hopped up immediately while others dawdled, but all were ready by four o'clock in either coats and boots or with their bag to go down to the daycare center. Normally Mandy would be picking with her students and being generally silly about the day as they waited to release them to their parents. Today she'd been distracted by her parents, Ashton, and where her life was headed. She'd be happy following her friends' lead and accepting the choices. It wasn't like she was nearing retirement—nothing she'd done would damage her forever. In fact, thanks to Mary Beth and Gabbie, she was better off than she could have ever been.

Parents checked in with her on their child's progress or the day's events. Smiling, she answered and tried to be cordial without jumping out of her skin. Was this what the others went through knowing they'd see the person they love at the end of the day? Love. How the fuck did that word jump into her mind.

"Moron," she grumbled, only to come out of her thoughts by a shocked parent.

"What was that, Ms. Mand?"

"I'm sorry, Mrs. Jones, what was your question again?"

"Did Cannon give you my note?"

"Yes." She shook her head. "Sorry, yes, and I'm sorry to hear about your family's loss."

"Right, well, I suppose you're all a little unsure around here with Sarah's friend having no result yet in the election."

"We are a bit." Mandy caught herself when she saw Ash walk into the waiting area. She gave him a side eye, wondering why he'd show up here.

"Oh my," Mrs. Jones said as she looked over her shoulder and caught a glimpse of Ash in his worn out jeans, tight, light blue V-neck sweater, and a gray skull cap. His blue eyes sparkled all the way across the hall, and Mandy had to control her own urges. "Being married sucks sometimes."

"Being single isn't the best thing in the world either," Mandy assured her, and walked over to Ash, careful to keep her distance. "I thought you were meeting me at my place, not here."

"I was tasked with one more Karen chore." He held up a messenger bag that looked really familiar.

"Thank you, Ash," Sarah said from behind her as she took the bag and slung it across her body. "I can't believe I forgot that. With Karen at her parents' place for the next few days I get to have a break and hang out with Mandy."

"Is that really less stressful than Karen?" Ash asked, not taking his eyes from Mandy's.

"By about sixty points," Sarah said as she put her arm around Mandy's shoulder. "Now, please say there's a reunion show on tonight."

"Nope." Mandy tried to hide her disappointment. "But there's a new show premiering. *The Naked Life*. It's about a nudist colony in central Florida."

"Seriously?"

"Yeah, I think it's a spin off of some Amish show."

"Now you're just joking with me."

"No…I'm not. If they could get a DJ or professional athlete, it might hit the trifecta."

"Things will be blurred out."

"If by things you mean…" Mandy looked for little ears. Finding none, she continued, "Cock, pussies, and tits, yes, things will be blurred."

"Please say I can come over." Ash laughed with a huge smile.

"Why would I spend a second more in your presence than necessary?"

"Because secretly you're in love with me."

"That wasn't love, that was gas. I could see how you could get that confused."

"Oh snap," Sarah exclaimed as she took off down the hall. "I forgot Margie needed me to put her stuff in the kiln before I left."

"Who's Margie?" Ash asked.

"A student."

"Since we're alone again," Ash began making the same location sweep as before, only with an eyebrow wiggle that made Mandy's lip turn up at the side. "I guess I won't get to see you before I fly out."

"Nope."

"And you won't take me to the airport."

"Not unless it's the only safe location during a zombie apocalypse, but I doubt they'd still be flying."

"Maybe instead of brains they want overpriced, watered down liquor."

"Who doesn't?" Mandy scoffed and the unease she felt when she was close to Ash in a public place set in. Her skin scratched against her clothing and she heard every noise. Her stomach clenched and her face felt flushed, she feared someone beside Gabbie catching her. "Well, I have to close down my classroom."

"Right, and I have to go home and pack."

Mandy rocked back on her heels and headed to her classroom. When her hand was on the door she turned to see if he'd moved. He hadn't. He was staring at her.

"If you were to…you know, text me or call not during school hours…I'd…well…it wouldn't be a bad thing."

"Because you secretly love me," he cooed and winked at her.

"No, you just don't make me vomit anymore."

~ * ~

Are you naked? Ash shot a text to Mandy.

No, but everyone on my screen is.

I'm naked.

Are you in central Florida? I could try to catch a glimpse.

He decided to reel the flirting in a little.

I can't believe this show is real.

I feel sorry for Mitzy.

I feel sorry for the production crew who have to see her without the blur strips.

Mandy didn't respond for a few minutes, and he used the time to scroll through his emails. Snatching his extra pillow from the other side of the bed, he stuffed it behind his head and the smell of Mandy's shampoo came off the case. Inhaling deeply, he tried to place the combination.

What scent is your shampoo?

Cotton blossom, why?

Couldn't place it.

Are you sniffing something of mine like a stalker?

He couldn't hold himself back anymore.

Your stench has invaded my room. Must have been when you were bent in half mid climax.

They have this new invention, a washing machine.

You wash your sheets yet?

In hot water with the strongest bleach known to man.

So, no, he replied.

No, but just because I'm lazy.

Of course, not because you want to snuggle with a pillow that reminds you of me.

He added an emoticon and immediately wanted to pull it back. What man sends a winky smiley face sticking out its tongue?

I love my roomy, but right now I actually wish you were here.

I won't tell...but what would we be doing?

I'm not sure about you, but DeDe and Joe seem to have good ideas.

Ash looked back at the TV to see the cast members Mandy was talking about.

Between the two of us, you'd be the one on all fours with a collar. He texted.

Promise.

The emoticon she sent to him was x-rated and he assumed was a download because there was no way a keyboard could make that shape. The politician in him was being beaten back by the horny teenager ready for nude pics and sexting. When his phone rang, the politician won out.

"Ashton Gilmore," he answered.

"Hey Ash, it's Victor, slight change in plans for tomorrow."

"How's that?" Ash asked, trying to avoid the ping from a text message.

"I'm going to have you meet me at the Colonial Club for a breakfast meeting."

"I don't get in until ten thirty." Ping.

"Oh, I also bumped your flight. Don't worry, I booked you a suite, but you'll need to get to the airport like twenty minutes ago. You're flying out at ten forty-five."

"Seriously?" Ash balked as he looked at his watch. It was already seven thirty-six. "Well, I guess it's a good thing I packed."

"Great, I'll shoot you the details. You fly out of terminal one instead of two."

"I'll call for a cab right now. See you in the morning."

Ash called for a cab then tossed his phone on the bed. Scrambling, he pulled together the last of his travel kit and headed for the lobby of his condo. Luckily downtown St. Paul had a pretty steady amount of cab traffic and as he walked out the one he'd ordered was waiting for him.

His phone pinged again and he scrolled through Mandy's messages.

Will I have to bite a rubber ball too or will you have something more substantial for my mouth?

Fuck me. Ash ran his fingers through his hair.

What, no offers?

Magilla?

He pumped all his diplomatic skills into his response.

Sorry, sexy, got a call and flying out in a few hours not in the morning. Any chance you'd want to stay up late and help me get to sleep?

No, came back immediately.

Think for a minute.

His phone beeped and booped from her typing for over a minute.

No.

Did I do something wrong?

I'm not on all fours with you buried deep inside of me. I'm eating pistachio ice cream watching blurred out naked people.

So, what you're saying is you miss me?

I have my pillow, she texted back.

He smiled as he took the fifteen-minute ride to the airport. Before he boarded the plane, he sent one last text.

I will miss you.

A car was waiting for him when he arrived. Even though he was exhausted, the buzz in the air in Washington D.C. shot through his body like a jolt of pure adrenaline had been stabbed into his heart. There was something about the city that made him feel alive every time he was there. By the time he got to Capitol Hill he'd be bursting at the seams. The history, the power, the movement, and rush of it all was intoxicating. He knew why Karen so desperately wanted to be there. Sure, inside the State House there was a bit of a buzz. People moving here and there. But in D.C., despite its light blanket of snow, the city was alive.

Even at night, the sight of monuments lit up had a tingle running down Ash's spine. He was falling in love with Washington and all it stood for. As he passed the Lincoln Memorial, he remembered his phone and turned it back on. Dinging and buzzing, it updated him on all his missed emails, phone calls, and texts, but there was only one grabbing his attention.

I'll miss you more than air.

You hate air. Ash smiled as he texted Mandy back.

Like you, Magilla, it's grown on me.

You're still up?

Cupcake Explosion had a marathon.

Go to bed, Mandy, the couch will hurt your neck.

It's too empty and Sarah won't snuggle with me...the prude.

Ashton sighed at the mention of snuggling as his side warmed in remembrance of the feel of Mandy against his bare flesh. The soft curves that melded to his body as if they were a matching set of tacky, old salt and pepper shakers.

Since when do you snuggle? Ash replied as he tried to shake off the domestic vision running amuck in his mind.

Caught the habit from a friend. What can I say, you've infected me with girl cooties you pussy.

How about after I check in I call you and help you tuck in by yourself?

There are worse things in the world than you singing me a lullaby.

Obviously, Mandy, you've never heard me sing.

Chapter Nine

"Flirting is the gentle art of making a man feel pleased with himself."
—Helen Rowland

By the time Mandy got home from work the next day, she was exhausted. Ash had kept her up way past her bedtime. He had to be just as tired as she was. With the time change, a breakfast meeting, and a fully packed day, she expected him to be ready to pass out just like her. Instead he called the moment she plopped on the couch.

"Hello, Amanda." A chill tore through her body, perking her nipples and making her breasts ache to be held. Something about him just saying her full name could turn her on.

"Ashton."

"You sound tired."

"I don't live the life of luxury you do. Driving home was a bit too much for me."

"Because of the bumper to bumper traffic on McKnight?" he teased.

"Something like that." She stretched out on the couch and held a throw pillow to her chest. "Are you done for the day?"

"Nope, fundraising has no off season here. There's a dinner. I have to wear a tux."

"You have a tux?"

"I do now. I usually just rent one, but the discretionary budget had enough to buy me a cheap one."

"Please tell me it's pastel and has ruffles."

"In my dreams," Ash laughed. "Want me to take a selfie and show you?"

"Do you know how to take a picture of yourself with your shirt on and not in a bathroom mirror?"

"No, I guess I don't. I mean I'm not even wearing a baseball cap sideways."

"Then no."

"I could wear it home and you'd see it when you picked me up from the airport."

"Did you go to DC or an alternative universe?"

"You have to explain this fear of the airport."

Mandy huffed. "I don't fear the airport, I just don't want to be a dork standing with a piece of poster board and a bouquet of flowers outside of security."

"You know you can just pull up to the curb, and I'll come outside."

"And be hassled every two minutes by airport cops? No thank you. I hate the idea of doing loops until you finally come outside."

"Tell me about your day while I get dressed."

Mandy could tell he switched his phone to speaker and now she wished they'd Skyped so she could watch him strip down and put on a tux. Why was a man in a well cut suit sexier than butt naked? Especially with Ash—he didn't wear suits, they wore him.

She told him the stories of the kids and how she had to leave an area before bursting out laughing. She flipped her phone to speaker so she could start to cook and continue her day. Her thoughts flowed freely as she browned meat and loaded the dishwasher.

"You know it's funny when I'm in my classroom I'm never tired and I'm happy." Mandy stirred the hamburger meat and smiled at the relaxation she found in the simple domestic action of cooking. "I deal with the youngest age in the school. They haven't had a filter placed in them."

"Basically, you know where you stand with them, unlike the rest of the world," Ashton offered.

"Says the politician whose whole job is to lie."

"I haven't lied to you."

"Lie by omission."

There was a pause. "When did I lie to you?"

"When I first met you at the fair."

"At the fair? You mean when you were flashing your cleavage at Karen hoping to make her jump you?"

"I was proving a point and failed. It's happened once before."

"What? That you proved a point?" Ash gloated. "Or that you failed."

"And you wonder why I love my classroom," Mandy grumbled as she drained the fat from the skillet and added the noodles, sauce packet, and milk.

"Amanda Butler's happy place."

"Jealous?" she asked, but wasn't really sure in which way she meant it.

"A bit," Ash sighed. "I was hoping your happy place might include a six-two blond."

"You know about Gemini?" she teased while stirring the box meal. "I swear one night at the Townhouse…"

"You're hilarious." Mandy could hear him shuffling around a little faster now. "I have to go. My car is downstairs."

"Ooohhh, your car, so fancy."

"I'll be out late."

"In politician speak," Mandy said with her voice deep like Ash's. "You're on your own tonight."

"I'll try to call you in the morning."

"I'm not that needy." She sighed.

"Yeah, but you're smiling. Night, Amanda."

Mandy tried to drop her smile, but couldn't as she hung up the phone.

"Who was that?" Sarah asked, scaring Mandy so badly the skillet flew. Her supper went up into the air and over the two women. Wiping the yellow sauce off her face, Sarah composed herself. "You can throw all the food on me you want, you still can't lick me."

"Of course not, it's not done." Mandy laughed, happy that she'd just added the sauce and it wasn't scalding.

"Pizza or Chinese?" Sarah asked as she reached for the paper towels.

The girls cleaned up, ordered Chinese, and each took a shower while waiting on the delivery guy. Finally settled in their pajamas and hair tucked in towel turbans, the girls sat down to eat out of boxes.

"You still haven't told me," Sarah said while balancing her sesame chicken between her chopsticks.

"Was there a question floating in the air?"

"Who was on the phone?" Sarah asked then held a pillow up to avoid the spray of food.

"Very funny."

"Holy crap," Sarah exclaimed. "You like someone."

"Oh yeah," Mandy mocked. "I'm in love."

Mandy's phone buzzed, and Sarah stared at her. Mandy was reduced to having to rub her middle finger and thumb to quell her need to check it. It couldn't be Ash, she told herself. He was at a party. Her boyfriend was a very important person after all. He wouldn't have time for—

The word rattled around in her head like she was speaking a foreign language. Maybe she should Google the strange word. Surely, she'd get an answer.

"That wasn't my phone that buzzed," Sarah said.

"Are you sure?" Mandy asked, grabbing her phone, thankful Sarah had given her an out.

You know what I wish?

Mandy smirked as her thumbs typed a response.

That I was spread eagle naked in front of you with chocolate sauce and a can of whipped cream?

You know what else I wish?

That a blowjob was our standard greeting?

"Holy shit, you're in love," Sarah exclaimed.

"Am not," Mandy whined like one of her students as her face flushed and the phone buzzed again. "I'm going to my room."

"Mandy and the phone guy sitting in a tree," Sarah sang after her.

I'm sure we could initiate that policy change, but no, still not what I'm thinking.

Fine, what are you thinking? Warning, I probably won't care if it's not one of those two things.

I wish you were here with me. The women here are all dressed up, but I think you would blow them away.

Ash was laying it on thick. Not that she minded.

I'm not exactly the politician wife type.

Wife? I like the sound of that.

Mandy flopped her head on her pillow and closed her eyes until her phone vibrated again.

Sorry, didn't mean to scare you.

You can't scare me. Basically, I'm not the one you want if you need to make a good impression.

I'd still prefer you because you don't hold your tongue.

Speaking of tongues…

* * * *

Ash shifted in the banquet chair at the round table. He was trying to keep the stone face he'd honed over years on the campaign trail, but Mandy wasn't making it easy. Who knew a text description of the way he tasted could be so in depth. He almost thought she liked him for more than teasing purposes.

"Damn, she must be hot," Vic said as he slapped Ash on the back and took the seat next to him.

"Um, I was checking Hannity's tweets."

"Right, because politicos make you shift in your seat."

Ash realized there was no fooling a fellow professional bullcrapper. "Okay, there is someone."

"If someone hacked your phone, would it make the rounds?"

"I'm nobody, so I'd say no."

"You're nobody now," Victor said as he leaned forward on the table. "We brought you here to consult, but…well, we've started a file on you."

"I'm behind the scenes."

"For now. But a few political action committees are interested in having you head them for a year or two. Then the Senate seat is open in your state."

"It's not open, we have an incumbent."

"If you help him cover up some things," Victor said as he spun his glass so the ice clinked. "Ignoring his call for help will keep our party pure and him out of office I guess."

"Pure? What exactly does that mean?"

"Let's just say we are supposed to be the party of good Christians who follow the tenets of God."

"Funny." Ash sat back in his seat. "Karen's biggest thing was small government and helping people be self sufficient instead of dependent on the government."

"Karen's a lesbian."

"And conservative," Ash shot back. "Sex has nothing to do with values."

"Yes, yes it does."

"Right, because the conservatives caught with hookers are okay."

Vic adjusted his tie and looked Ash straight in the eye. "They lost our support."

"And the ones who've cheated on their wives, but married the mistress. They're okay, right?"

"Now come on."

"Karen's getting married, once. How many of your purest on the Hill can you say that about?"

"You don't know that for sure…"

"Actually, I do. I know more than the press releases on her. I know her as a person and at all these meetings today I thought that was what you wanted me to do. Get a feel for the person."

"You can't get the feel for a person here," Victor laughed. "You guys from the fly over states are so funny when you first get here."

"Right, Minnesota doesn't matter. Maybe that's why the Republicans haven't won it in forever. You mock Iowa's straw poll even though you know you need their support to win the election. Ohio, is that still a fly over state? This country is more than the coasts. You called me, I didn't call you. You called because I have something you don't anymore—integrity. A sense of right and wrong."

"You lied for almost a decade, was that right?"

"No, that was me being you." Ash stood and straightened out his jacket. "But unlike you, I've learned from my mistakes."

"Finally, someone with enough balls to tell Vic to shove it," a gruff man's voice said as a hand appeared. "Troy Graves, I'm stupidly trying to be the chair next year."

"Let me guess, you dress in women's clothes." Ash stood his ground and didn't shake the man's hand.

"Nah, the lace chafes too much. Shake my hand, son."

Ash gave in and received a strong handshake.

"You must be Ashton Gilmore," Troy sighed. "It's not that I want to deal with Victor, but I have to. I'd rather work with you. I don't believe in the cleansing of the party. I want to set forth a platform for those who agree with the Republicans."

"What a crazy idea." Ash smirked.

"Sit down, Vic will fetch you a drink, and I'll tell you the real reason you're here."

Troy laid out a plan Ash prayed wasn't a chess move. Then again, wasn't politics just a giant game of chess? Not with Karen. She was still innocent enough to believe in the system. She actually read the bills.

"Look, we have quite a few months before we'd need you for a permanent position," Troy said as the night wore on and Ash noticed the ballroom had emptied. "This is just a temporary position to start with. We'd hope to build up your work here and in Minnesota. You've got everything necessary to win a Senate seat."

"That was Karen's wish."

"She was on track for it. Now I'm not sure. We're not pulling our support yet. It's all up to her votes. Historically she has more party line votes than most."

"I believe she's only not voted the line once in the last three years."

"She abstained a few times."

"Who hasn't? Those were times when her constituency would have been hurt with either choice."

"You have been paying attention. Who was really in charge in that office?"

"Her. She believes in government more than anyone I've ever met."

"More than you?"

Ash drummed his fingers on the table. Coming to DC had removed his blinders. It was easy to believe in the system in Karen's office. She never wavered. She's the one who should be getting a Senate seat offered, not him. He'd need her on his staff if he won.

"I've come out here a handful of times. I've seen the man behind the curtain."

"What do you think of him?"

"That years ago he believed, and if he would again, this country would be better off."

* * * *

"Tell me it isn't true." Jillian stood at Mandy's door with tears streaming down her face. The youngest of Mandy's sisters had the rich red hair of Grace, her mother. Although Mandy had no idea why she was here. "Tell me, Mandy."

"The tooth fairy will not give you triple for wisdom teeth."

"Not now."

"Okay, you're right, Jilly Bean, come in." Mandy stepped back and Jillian headed straight to the kitchen. Mandy poked her head into the hallway looking for Mary Beth or someone. Sarah came out of her room. The loud pounding from Jill had probably woken more than the two of them.

"Hey, Jill," Sarah greeted her and began rubbing circles on her back.

"You okay?"

"No," she choked the word out. "No, I'm not okay."

"What happened?" Mandy asked the sobbing Jill as she cleared the mail from the counter.

"Is your mother having my dad's baby?"

A chill shot up Mandy's back as both she and Sarah took a step back. The air was sucked out of the room.

"What makes you—"

"They were fighting. Mom and Dad. And then I heard Mom yell about your mom." Jillian's eyes were blood shot and her face flushed. "Did my dad get your mom pregnant?"

"It's not like it's the first time," Mandy snipped, partially because she'd actually fallen asleep before being rudely awakened. Having siblings sucked sometimes.

Sarah's eyes got wide as she cocked her head to the side.

"What?" Mandy grumbled at Sarah. "Screw this, I'm tired of the lies."

"What do you mean it's not the first time?" Jillian gasped. "You don't have any siblings."

"Well...that's not a hundred percent true." Mandy settled herself across from Jillian. "We found out last year that I'm your sister."

Jillian's flushed face lost all its color. Instead of the splotchy redness brought on by tears, now only freckles colored her pale skin. Mandy covered Jill's hands with hers and let the knowledge wash over her.

"Is that why Mom let Mary Beth come home?" she asked.

"Partially. We both wanted to tell you, but couldn't. I'm sorry you found out this way."

"Who else knows? Carry? Gwen? Wills?"

"Just Mary Beth. Didn't she bring you? How did you get here? I'm not mad you came, but you're only fifteen."

"I stole my mom's car."

"Okay." Mandy woke more at that little tidbit. "Let me call her to let her know you're okay."

"Fuck her."

"Hey," Mandy snapped. "She's your mother and has put up with a lot over the years."

"With how she treated you, you defend her."

"She's still your mother and loves you very much."

"They're getting a divorce, aren't they?" Jillian gulped back a hard breath of air.

"They've been getting divorced for twenty-five years if you hear my mom tell it." Mandy squeezed Jill's hands and their eyes locked. The hazel eyes from their father matched almost perfectly. "Jill, the only good thing that came from all of this was getting wonderful brothers and sisters. Now, I'm going to call your mom before she completely loses it."

Mandy made the call she never wanted to make to Grace Wallace, the woman who'd tormented her for over half her life.

"Grace," Mandy said after she answered the phone. "It's Mandy, I just wanted to let you know Jill's at my apartment."

"Jill?" Panic filled Grace's voice. "She's not in her room?"

"No, ma'am, I guess she overheard you and Kevin discussing...well...you know what you were fighting about."

"Your mother and...and...the baby."

"I'm sorry about that."

"How did she get there?"

"Your car."

"She's just got her permit! She can't drive."

"I figure that's a mom thing to deal with. I'll see if Mary Beth can come over and get her back home without breaking the law."

There was an uncomfortable silence and just as Mandy was about to hang up, Grace coughed.

"Thank you, Amanda. I suppose Jillian now knows the whole truth."

"She knows I'm her sister."

"Well, another secret that shouldn't have been kept, I suppose." Grace sniffed a bit. "I loved him once. I really did. Do you think he ever loved me?"

"I think he still does in his own twisted way."

"Eli's not like that with Mary Beth, is he?"

"She learned her lesson with Nate and wouldn't allow it."

"I guess it is kind of my fault. I knew about your mother and didn't object. I was raised to make the home and the man would be there. He only wandered if the home was out of balance."

"Have you learned that's bullshit?"

"Yes…yes I have."

"Good. Now I've got a half sister in shock I need to tend to."

"Let her spend the night if she needs it. There are worse things than skipping church."

"All right, and Grace," Mandy said.

"Yes."

"Take it all in the divorce. Everything you see, and know, and dig for what might be hidden."

Chapter Ten

"I don't have a girlfriend. But I do know a woman who'd be mad at me for saying that."
—Mitch Hedberg

"Where are we going?" the cab driver asked as Ash slid in the back.

The only address that came to mind was Mandy's.

"Maplewood," he said, then proceeded to give the address.

It was almost ten-thirty, so Ash didn't think he needed to knock too lightly. If nothing else, Mandy should be preparing for the high holy day that was football. As the door opened, he wondered who had the rougher night.

Mandy's eyes were hooded and her dark hair tumbled down to her breasts. She wore a long T-shirt with a baby chick wearing glasses that said *nerd chicks are hot*. It came to mid-thigh, and he wondered if she was wearing panties. All he could think about was slamming her against the wall, lifting her by her hips, and spreading her thighs.

Instead he ran his hand along her cheek and crushed his lips against hers. The sweet taste of pistachio ice cream filled his senses and he knew she'd had a hard night. She clawed at his shoulders and even though he wanted to find out what had her upset last night, he knew this was helping her more.

"We need to talk," she gasped when they'd finally broken the embrace and she pushed him out into the hallway.

"Okay."

"Are you sleeping with anyone else?"

The accusation slapped him.

"No," he replied. Fear gripped his heart. She was about to tell him what she'd done. "I mean we never said we were exclusive…"

"But neither of us is sleeping with anyone else either." Relief washed over him at her comment. "Are you like…are we…are you my boyfriend?"

"Um, I…"

"It's just…we aren't going out and picking up anyone else. We talk and text all the time. It seems like a…" Her finger spun a few times as her head cocked to the side. "Relationship."

"Do you want to be my girlfriend? You said before you didn't like labels."

"What exactly would that mean?"

Ash stumbled trying to explain what a normal relationship would mean. What was a normal relationship? And could Mandy even do that?

"I like what we're doing, so is there something else that would change? A requirement or something?"

"Well, most relationships aren't hidden. I mean, besides Gabbie, who knows we even spend time together?"

"Like a declaration?" she asked.

"I don't think we need to rent a plane to write it in the sky, but um…I guess it would be nice to actually kiss a girl in public."

Mandy took his hand in hers and dragged him in the apartment. A shower was running as she opened the bathroom door.

"Sarah," she called.

"Ah, boundaries," she called from in the shower.

"Please," Mandy scoffed. "Ash and I have been sleeping together for months now. He's like my…boyfriend or some such thing."

The curtain pulled back a bit and Sarah poked her head out. Her blonde hair was slicked back. At first, she only saw Mandy. When Ashton came into her line of sight her eyes opened wide.

"This couldn't of waited until I got out of the shower?"

"Why are you taking another shower? I guess I could have waited. Maybe…anyway. Just wanted to declare it or something."

"Okay, your social skills are a bit lacking. Thanks for the update, but I knew that."

"You did not."

"Right, you hate him more than air, his cologne is usually wafting from your room, and you aren't having an *Aspirin* smoothie every morning."

"You suck," Mandy spat. "Who else knows?"

"How would I know?"

They left the bathroom and she pulled him into her bedroom where Mary Beth was passed out with a younger redhead curled up next to her.

"Yo," Mandy called. The girls moved a bit but didn't wake until Mandy tossed a stress ball from her dresser and pegged Mary Beth on the head.

"What's your issue, Butler?" Mary Beth snapped, and then caught sight of Ashton. "Oh, um…"

"He's my boyfriend." Mandy pointed to Ash. "Let me guess, you already knew?"

Mary Beth rolled her eyes, and Ash stifled his grin. Mandy immediately turned around and fled. Ash wasn't sure what had just happened.

Mandy turned into a cleaning lady as she wandered back into the kitchen. She started scrubbing dishes, and then stopped and put them into the dishwasher. Ashton pulled a bunch of spoons out of empty containers of ice cream.

"Bad night?" he asked after tossing four empty quart cartons of pistachio ice cream into the trash.

"Jillian found out about my mom, me, well, the whole mess."

"Jillian? The little redhead in there?" he asked.

"Yes, I had to have Mary Beth come over because she stole her mom's car and, well…it was a long night."

"That's why you look so tired."

"You didn't help with that," she said with a smirk. "How was your flight?"

"Good. I came straight from the airport."

"That explains the bag."

He pointed one of the ice cream stained spoons at her. "What was with the Ashton's-my-boyfriend-parade?"

"You're my first anything. If I did it wrong, then I'll know better for the next one."

"What if there isn't a next one?"

"Oh God, are you going back to that stupid wife comment?" She grabbed the spoons out of his hand and started rinsing them off. Her hands were shaking a little. "Because if you are, then I'll have another parade, the Ashton's-not-my-boyfriend."

Instead of finding her insanity annoying, he'd begun to find it adorable. He was so screwed.

* * * *

"Exactly how serious is this thing with you and Ash?" Sarah asked as they were all in Gabbie's office sharing lunch.

"I called him my boyfriend," Mandy replied, unsure where she was going. "Why do I need to define it more than that?"

"You're not dating anyone else?" Gabbie said.

"I'm not really dating him. We're just not sleeping with other people."

"How are you not dating him?" Sarah asked.

"I've heard of dates, they involve more than sex and food."

"Not really," Gabbie said while stabbing a piece of chicken in her salad. "I mean you go out to eat, and then have sex, right?"

"Um, there are other aspects," Mary Beth said as she bit into her sandwich.

"Are there any that matter?" Mandy asked. "Because food and sex are pretty much the only basic human needs."

"What are you teaching my children?" Gabbie asked.

"Do they help you with dishes and laundry?" Mandy asked, but didn't wait for a response. "You're welcome."

"It's just strange," Mary Beth said. "You aren't the biggest proponent of monogamy."

"Strange with all the wonderful examples of what it means." Mandy popped a few chips in her mouth. "How's Jill?"

"Better than Carry, I didn't think he'd take it so hard."

Carrington was a senior in high school and should be focused on picking his college, not this crap. Only Jill had contacted her, and although she didn't want to be hurt, she had been. What had she expected? They'd run to her and been excited to not only have a new sister, but one more on the way.

"Do, um…can I help?" Mandy asked. Mary Beth pursed her lips and twisted them to the side. "Right, too soon."

"Mom's really pushing for the divorce now, and since Minnesota's a no-fault state it should go quickly. It's not like Dad can fight it, and I guess she's done. I think he moved in with your mom."

"I haven't heard. Somehow my mom's number is blocked on my phone," Mandy confessed with no remorse. "Am I being childish?"

"A bit, but you deserve a few days not living a reality TV show," Sarah said as she looked at the clock. "I guess we better get back to our rooms."

Sarah put her arm around Mandy as they both walked toward their rooms. Mandy rested her head on Sarah's shoulder. Touching had usually been restricted, but now she craved it. The warmth of a body next to her. Arms surrounding her. Things that previously made her skin crawl now calmed her. Begrudgingly, she had to admit that a week of Ash being able to hold her most nights had shifted her focus.

"If Karen wins she'll want Ash to go with her. I know he hasn't been doing much," Sarah said. "I'm sure he wants a job again."

"But he is working."

"He is?" Sarah asked as they stood in the vestibule that separated off into their respective hallways. "Where?"

"If he hasn't told Karen, then it's probably not for me to share," Mandy said and headed down to her classroom. If there was one thing Mandy had perfected over the years, it was holding just enough of a secret to keep her from being culpable.

As Mandy settled into her afternoon lessons, she chose a handful of kids to go over the sandpaper alphabet. The five she chose took different positions on the floor. Two were on their bellies, two sat on their knees, and the final one, Claire, lay on her back thinking she'd hold the thin, wooden board upside down.

"Claire," Mandy said, patiently. "If we were writing in the air you'd be in the perfect position, but I need you to at least roll over."

"I can do it, Ms. Mand," she stated proudly as she held the thin board with the letter T on it above her head and traced it.

"But what about when I need you to copy the motion in the sandbox." Mandy tapped the edges of the box with a thin layer of sand in the bottom.

"Oh," Claire replied with her face screwed into a sideways O. "But…if I sits on my knees my pretties will gets holes."

Claire's pretties, aka her tights, held a place somewhere ranking among gold for the most precious objects on earth. Poor Gabbie had adopted a girly girl when Gabbie had barely registered as female for most of high school. The learning curve on dresses, sparkly shoes, and hair ribbons had been high, but fortunately not insurmountable, and now Gabbie took to being the mother of a girl with gusto.

"Claire, may I suggest sitting like I am." Mandy demonstrated how to sit down and keep her legs to the side. "This way your pretties won't get damaged."

Complying with her wishes, Claire switched her posture and they began the lesson. When they were all done, the children put away the materials and Mandy's body groaned as she pushed up from the floor. A light tapping on her window made her turn to see Jillian outside her classroom. The children, curious about the interruption in their quiet afternoon, rushed behind Mandy who had to instruct them to return to their work.

"'tis that Auntie Mary Bef's sister?" Claire asked.

"Yes, Claire, that's Jillian," Mandy said as she placed her hands on Claire's shoulders and turned her around. "Now I need to have a discussion with her on how to use a door."

"She's too big to not know that."

"You're right, but I think she'll learn."

Mandy opened her window and looked at her little sister.

"Why aren't you in school?"

"I took the driver's ED car. I just couldn't sit in school anymore."

"Okay, grand theft auto. Awesome. How about you come in the front door and we sit down and talk?"

"I just wanted the keys to your apartment. I can't live at home anymore. I knew Mary Beth would lecture me."

"And my house seemed the best fit?"

"I can't live with Mary Beth and Luke, Sarah's moving out soon.

Can I please live with you?"

"Are you going to steal my car if I say no?"

Jillian gave her a grimace that reminded Mandy of Mary Beth. Maybe it's not a mom thing, but a Wallace trait.

"Come inside," Mandy said and gave Jillian the code so she wouldn't have to have Mary Beth buzz her in. "It's freezing out, and I'm sure the cops are hunting you right now."

Jillian found her way to Mandy's classroom and peeked her head inside.

"They're all so little," she cooed. "Where's Luke?"

"He's a first grader, he's with Sarah."

"That's Claire and Charlie, right?"

When she stepped further into the room Mandy stopped her. Over the years no one would ever accuse Mandy of being the grown up of the group. She'd never been tasked with such duties. Basically, she was the enforcer and party planner, but Jillian was making her switch roles.

"First, stop stealing cars—"

"Sometimes I just need to get away. You know that feeling, right?"

"Yes, but you already have two very good ways to get away. Your right and left leg. A brisk walk is a better avenue and less of a felony."

Mandy escorted Jillian back out into the cubby room after nodding to Jasmine she'd be stepping out. No reason to declare the adjustment and cause the kids to react.

"So can I?" Jillian asked as her eyes pooled with tears and pain reflected in her features. Her sister for only a week and still the similarities were striking. "I have nowhere else to go. My friends can't take me in and none of them can understand what we're going through."

Mandy pulled her little sister into her arms and held tight. Jillian was reserved like Mary Beth, the way all the Wallace children were raised. Tiny cries sounded in her ear that could have been confused for a newborn child. All Mandy could do was cradle her head against her shoulder and rock back and forth. Her body warmth creating a sensation of safety.

"Everything's gone," she croaked. "It's all been a lie."

"No, it hasn't. Jilly Bean, your mom and dad love you."

"Dad doesn't know love."

"He loves in a different way than others."

"I know how he loves." She snuffed and pulled away.

"Your mom needs you even more now. Trust me, baby sister."

"You called me your sister," she said with a smile when she pulled back, her eyes rimmed red.

"I've called you that before."

"No, you told me I was your sister, but you never just called me one."

"Well, you are," Mandy said and smoothed back her loose red hair. "I love you, Jilly, always have. That's saying a lot because I can't stand Gwen."

"No one can stand her."

"You know you're in trouble, right?"

"What did she do this time?" Mary Beth snapped as she came into the room.

"I'll take care of it," Mandy said.

"Because you're involved once again." Mary Beth stood with her arms crossed.

"Excuse me?" Mandy shoved Mary Beth into the hallway and the women locked eyes. "I know a cop, I'll handle Jill."

"You know a cop," Mary Beth snarled. "Of course you know a cop, but what does a cop need with my sister?"

"Our sister, and I'll take care of it."

"I'm older by three months, so how about you give me an idea of what's going on."

"Jill is standing in the cubby room crying and you're accusing me and trying to butt in where you're not wanted."

The slap echoed in the quiet hallway. It even bounced all the way down to the one child who'd been using the bathroom. Sophie stood wide eyed with her two blonde ponytails balancing out her head. Both women stared back at her and Mandy held back the tear as it rested on the edge of her eye above the cheek that burned.

Slippered feet trailed down the hallway, and Mary Beth dropped to her knee to explain to the little girl. It was useless. There'd never be a good enough explanation that would make sense in her little world. Sophie clung to the wall for protection until she could reach Mandy.

Tousling her hair a bit, Mandy gave the assured look that let the child know she was okay. Sophie tottered back into the room with a freshly traumatized glaze on her face.

"We've got about four minutes before it's all over my classroom that you slapped me."

"I want to do so much more to you."

"Why? What have I done beside support you and your whole damn family?" Mandy stepped to Mary Beth, closing the space once more. "Jill showed up here because she knew I'd support her, unlike you."

"In what, a felony?"

"No, that the redheaded beast of the devil did herself. But because I love her I'll see what I can do to avoid her going to juvie."

"I could go to juvie?" Jillian asked as she came into the hallway. "What happened to your cheek?"

"Nothing," Mandy said as she covered it with her hand. "You didn't steal your mom's car, you stole the school's. Good chance they'll press charges."

"You stole the school's car!" Mary Beth cried, the pitch was slightly sharper than a group of howler monkeys.

"Stop," Mandy ordered and pushed them further from the classroom. "She screwed up. She's fifteen. She's allowed. Now take her to your office and let me make a phone call."

Mandy went back to her room and went to her supply closet to retrieve her phone. Jasmine poked her head in the closet.

"Hey, any direction?" Jasmine asked. Mandy looked at her phone. It was only one o'clock.

"When does E one have their gym time?" Mandy asked while pulling out the master schedule. "Take them either to the gym or bundle them up and let them have more recess time. I'm going to need you to stay past two and close down the classroom."

"Sure." Jasmine turned and redirected a student to return to work. "Is everything okay?"

"It will be, just a dash of drama that hopefully all the kids won't be bringing home."

Mandy scanned her phone for Drew's number. She pulled on her coat as the phone rang and she walked down to the office.

"Long time, sexy," Drew purred when he answered the phone. "Did I leave my handcuffs last time I was with you?"

"Um…possession is nine tenths of the law?"

"Oh man, you're killing me, Mandy. Something tells me I'll need to come over and frisk you for them later."

"Would that I could, but I'm in need of a different one of your skills."

"You peaked my interest…as well as other things."

"Things? Did you grow another one?" she teased and instantly felt guilty. Mary Beth was pacing in her office, surely giving Jillian the talking to of her life.

"You wish. So what do you need?"

"A myriad of things, but this is a big favor, and I'd owe you for it."

"Do I get to get creative when it comes to you paying me back?"

"Drew," she warned as her gut pulled in a bit.

"All right, sexy, what is it?"

"How about I meet you?"

"I'm at the station now."

"Okay, how about I'll come to Walton and maybe you and I can talk in the far parking lot."

"See you in a few. I was supposed to go on patrol soon anyway."

Mary Beth had her head on her desk and Jillian looked like she was in the principal's office instead of the billing department. As Mandy walked in, her head shot up.

"Please say you've crushed the car and made it disappear."

"Hmm…that's a grown up idea. I'm going to meet with a friend. Keep your cell phone on."

Mandy's history with Drew had never been more than flirting and fucking. He was three years older than her, and he'd met her as a freshman in high school. Unlike the other guys who were trying to score and move on, Drew protected her. Even stopped her from a potentially dangerous situation she found herself in at a party.

"How is that a good idea?" a deep voice asked Mandy as she turned the corner about to follow Conrad. She turned sharply on her heel and saw a guy with dark hair, light eyes, and lips about to surround a bottle

of water.

"What do you think I'm about to do?" she challenged with her hands resting on her hips.

"Well, Conrad just walked by so I'm assuming as an eighth grader you're eager to follow."

"I'm a freshman," she snapped.

"You look like an eighth grader who's trying too hard to fit in," he said as he stepped closer to her and the heat of his body surrounded her. His cologne and slight shadow of facial hair made her stomach clench at the upgrade. "Go home."

"I go to Tartan with you, so how about you stop being an asshat and let me go my own way."

"Following Conrad." His left eyebrow rose.

"Maybe."

"Because Conrad wasn't the only one who went in that room."

Mandy looked past the guy to the closed door.

"I have a better offer for you."

"Right, I'm sure, you do. I know Conrad, you're a stranger."

"I'm Drew, now you know as much about me as you do about Dixon."

"Who's Dixon?"

"Conrad Dixon."

"Oh, um…" Mandy's face flushed as she tried to hold on to her tough as nails persona.

"Do you have friends here?" he asked. "You know, a group you came with?"

"No, I came by myself."

"All right, fresh meat, you're coming with me."

"Right, that's safe."

"And going into a room, that probably locks, with three guys, one of which you just learned his last name…that's safe."

"Three?" Mandy asked as she swallowed the lump in her throat. Conrad knew she was still a virgin.

He'd promised to be gentle, make the experience special, and help her get past the stupid hump. Her mother had been lost in her own loneliness again and she refused to be like her. Moping over the first guy she'd been with—the only one Mandy knew of. The allure and fantasy of her father returning to the woman who'd held a candle for him all these years had Mandy about to skip down a hallway. Instead Drew held out his hand and redirected her. Much like Mary Beth's dad did when she was about to fly off the handle at an umpire or teammate for screwing something up.

"So, Mandy, how about I drive you home. This party blows," Drew offered as he placed an arm around her shoulder and turned her around. Looking over her back she saw Conrad standing with his arms crossed and just like Drew said, two of his buddies were on either side with the same pissed off look.

"Why are you looking out for me?" Mandy snapped. "You expect a blowjob or something?"

"Let's just say you'll owe me. I'll come up with something we both can agree on for payment." He opened the door to his car and buckled her seatbelt for her. "Mandy, there are two types of guys in the world. Predators and heroes. Not all predators are scary looking and not all heroes wear capes."

Drew nodded at her in school when he saw her in the hall the next week. He even slammed Conrad into the lockers the one time he walked toward her. If he'd been younger maybe he would have stopped her from the mistakes she made in later years, but he'd only had time to look after her freshman year. Still, it had made all the difference.

It came as no surprise to Mandy when he became a cop. He'd always understood her and known her limitations—never pressing them and never tossing on a cape and being captain save-a-ho. They were friends, eventually with benefits, but never more. She didn't commit to anyone, and he was fine with that.

"Hey stranger," he said as he got out of his cruiser to give her a hug. His lips brushed against her neck, but the normal reaction she'd always had wasn't there.

At six feet even, with broad shoulders and a square jaw, he'd been formidable on the football field. Now his bulk was a hundred percent muscle as all the fat of youth had conformed into the mold of a man. The only thing she missed was the five o'clock shadow he'd grow on his days off.

"Clean shaven," she teased as she held his chin in her hands. "So wrong."

"Are you?" he flirted back and she smacked his chest. "Oh man, you do want to be in cuffs, assaulting an officer of the law like that."

"Favor first, then we can discuss payment." Her hands slid down his arms as she leaned against her car and created space. He intertwined their fingers and twisted their arms around her back.

"All right, you've intrigued me."

"Remember the stupid shit we did in high school?"

"And by we you mean you." His eyebrow quirked up.

"If we're going to be dabbling in reality, you might not be the best choice for this discussion," she teased. He pressed his body against her, and then suddenly let go and stepped back right before another cruiser passed them. "Last year I came to you when I lost it."

"The whole Mary Beth thing?"

"Yes, and you stopped me from going off the deep end."

"And strained multiple parts of my body in the process."

"Please, after all these years you should know to stretch."

"True." Drew shifted his hips back and forth a few times.

"Her little sister Jillian just learned the truth after finding out the fun fact that my mom is pregnant."

"Shit," Drew said as he ran his hand over his face. "How are you? I mean your mom is knocked up."

"You know I had a meltdown, but not as severe. My…well…my friends helped me through." Mandy rocked back on her heels and stuffed her hands in her pockets. "Jillian is either too embarrassed, or doesn't have as good of a support system as I have."

"How big of a charge am I looking at?"

"Minor felony."

Drew let out a long breath of air, then clucked his tongue. His deep blue eyes wouldn't meet hers. Instead he looked at the parking lot, and she could see the calculations going off in his head.

"She goes to Tartan doesn't she?" he finally asked.

"Good guess." Mandy pursed her lips together knowing he'd figured it out.

"Where's the car now?"

"Safe, in St. Paul."

"How safe?"

"Let's say it could be parked by a lake."

"By or in?"

"By." They had a lake across the street from the school with a small parking lot and even if Jillian hadn't moved it there she would now.

"Between cameras and the fact only a handful of students skipped class means they'll figure out who stole the car. I don't think I can help you on this one."

"Please Drew. She's only fifteen and—"

His hand shot up and Mandy snapped her mouth shut.

"This isn't a speeding ticket, Mandy."

"I know. But Drew, this girl is my sister and obviously emotionally unstable because she thinks moving in with me would be smart."

His eyebrows shot up. That got his attention. "What lake is the car by?"

"Beaver, down by Edgewater and Magnolia."

"Dispatch, this is fifty-six," Drew said into the radio on his shoulder.

"Go ahead, fifty-six."

"Please contact St Paul and let them know we have a tip on the vehicle from Tartan. Look around Beaver Lake by Edgewater and Magnolia."

"Ten-four."

Drew crossed his arms over his chest.

"Call and have her leave the keys under the driver's seat and the door open. Just pray a patrol isn't nearby."

Mandy made the call and tried to calm Mary Beth down enough to relay the message.

"I don't know," Mandy spat and looked at Drew who was still standing with his arms crossed over his broad chest. "There are consequences in life."

"This is all your mom's fault," Mary Beth scolded.

"Okay, yeah, it's all her fault. Not our dad's or sister's, my mom spread her legs for an asshole she loves. How about I don't try to get Jill off?"

Mandy missed having a flip phone at the moment. Something about pressing end wasn't as satisfying as snapping a phone shut or slamming down the receiver. When her hand reared back Drew caught her wrist, and threw her against the car.

"I'll take this," he said, sliding her phone into his hand. "You can thank me later."

"How is this my fault again?"

"It's not."

"I thought Mary Beth had stopped blaming you for everything bad in the world."

"Oh please, you'll always be her favorite person to blame. Why look in a mirror when you can point across the room?"

The worst part of this whole thing wasn't that Drew may not be able to help Jill, but if he did, what she'd have to do for it. Being in a relationship did make getting out of trouble complicated. Her first thought when she learned what happened was Drew, not Ash, and that scared her. The girls didn't even know about Drew except as a passing overnight visitor.

"What's going to happen to Jill?"

"I'll go and talk to Principal Verner, maybe I'll be able to convince him we can sweep it under the rug."

"Just don't mention me."

"Why?"

"He taught social studies when we were in high school."

"Do I want to know?"

"Let's just say if I'm in the mix he may see things as genetic."

"Right," Drew said and kissed Mandy on the forehead. "I'll call you later. Will Jill be with you?"

"If that's what you want."

"Oh, my wants will be discussed later."

Chapter Eleven

"Life is all about timing."
—Carl Lewis

"I thought I was supposed to get a break during spring break?" Mandy whined as she and Ash carried more baby things into the nursery that was still far from complete. "Since when does Gabbie leave stuff to the last minute."

Ash laughed lightly as they finally got the crib into the bedroom.

"Why isn't Case helping us again?" Mandy yelled downstairs.

"Because I told him I would do it all."

"So you're not only an idiot, but a liar too."

Keeping a straight face around these two had become Ash's hardest job to date. Officially dating Mandy had been interesting. She'd never had a real relationship and although she understood the basics, he'd found dating her at times was like dating a sixteen-year-old.

The grown up thing was not her strong suit. When Gabbie called her in a panic he had to convince Mandy it was okay for him to tag along. His duty in a sense. Case had sent a text to Ash asking for help for some reason Gabbie had decided to go overboard since his grandmother's stroke. Luckily, he was on a break, too, and could help Mandy since Gabbie was eight months along and on restrictions.

Case had painted the nursery and set up a few things, but some of the furniture had been on backorder and magically showed up the day after he flew to Arizona.

"Hey, he had to go take care of his grandmother for a few days,"

Gabbie explained. "I didn't want to worry him."

"It's been a whole week." Mandy grunted as she and Ash carried a crib up the stairs. "You sure he isn't running out on you?"

"I'm telling him you said that. You know what he'll say?" Gabbie growled.

"That hormones had you hearing things and the baby is sucking out your smarts. Seriously, woman. I will deny anything you threaten right now."

"Guess what I'll do?" Gabbie snarled as she placed her hand on her side.

"See, even the interloper is on my side."

"Ha ha," Gabbie sarcastically replied, and Mandy rubbed the Buddha belly, cooing all the way.

"You love your Auntie Mand, don't you? Yes, you do, because Auntie Mand is the only one who loves you enough to deal with your mother."

"Ouch," Gabbie winced. "Quit teasing the animal, you taught him that, didn't you?"

"To kick you…hell yeah."

"Swear jar," Gabbie said, pointing out of the room. "Go on. Auntie Mand's mouth is paying for college."

With a huff, Mandy stormed out of the room after setting down the boxed furniture.

"Sorry you had to see that," Gabbie apologized. Ash waved her off.

"I've been in DC for the last two weeks, I've seen worse."

"That's good." Gabbie's pregnant glow lit up the room as she began to open the box. "Ash, how is she?"

"What do you mean?"

"You two are in a real relationship?" Gabbie waddled to the rocking chair in the corner and slowly lowered into it.

"For months now, what's so different this week?" He pulled out the parts and began reading the instructions.

"Because, she's never been in one."

"Well, we're virgins in that sense I guess. I've had a girlfriend here and there, but… let's just say Mandy and I are similar in many ways."

"Are you really?"

"Is he really what?" Mandy asked as she came back in the room.

"Hung like a horse. I swear sometimes your friends ask the strangest questions." Ash leaned to kiss Mandy on her forehead. It had taken awhile, but she'd finally learned to not pull away. "Have you been talking about me?"

"Please, I just show her the videos," Mandy said as she picked up the side rail and Gabbie winced again. "Now he's just being mean."

"That wasn't a kick." She scrunched her face and bit hard. "I think he's putting a media room in my uterus."

"I'm by far no expert on girl parts," Ash confessed, holding up his hands while Mandy winked and blushed. "But Karen has quite a few nieces and nephews."

"Your point?" Gabbie grimaced.

"You're great with child and having pains."

"I'm also not due for three more weeks."

"Oh, I forgot you plan everything and it never gets waylaid by life."

"Please say you're not saying what you're saying?" Mandy panicked as she started to shake her hands at her side like a tweener at a boy band concert.

"He's not because I won't let it happen," Gabbie insisted.

"Oh, well in that case I'll look for part A," Ash calmly replied in hopes sanity would set in before he found the right part.

Reality struck before sanity as Gabbie's leg shot straight out and she tried to bend over.

"Mandy, can you pass me that Allen wrench?" Ash asked calmly.

"Are you kidding me?" she balked.

"She's not having a baby," he pishawed and waved his hand. "She told me so. She didn't let her son know, but we know how those battles go."

"Should I call Case?" Mandy asked as she knelt by Gabbie who was breathing rhythmically.

"What if it's false labor?" she suggested. "I don't want him to rush home for nothing."

Ashton shook his head. "You're not nothing. Gabbie, come on. I'm calling Case and your dad."

"Okay," she nodded and tried to get up, only to have another contraction.

"These seem pretty close together. How long have you been having them?" Ash asked and was successful in extricating her from her chair.

"A few days."

"And you weren't worried."

"They weren't like this."

"They do tend to get stronger." Ash rolled his eyes. "What about Charlie and Claire?"

"They're in the daycare section of the school. Call Mary Beth."

"On it," Mandy replied as she unlocked her car door and they all piled in with Ash stealing the keys from Mandy.

"I'd like to get there in one piece. Which hospital?"

"United," Gabbie said. Ash headed for downtown St. Paul.

"Run every light," Mandy ordered. Ash laughed.

"Yeah, that's going to happen."

"Are you serious? I can't deliver a baby back here," Mandy squawked.

"When was her last contraction?" he asked.

"I don't know."

"That's your job right now. Keeping track of these things."

"When we left the house," she suggested.

"Gabbie?" he asked.

"A bit before that."

"Right," he said in a calm voice he'd mastered over the years, even though the fear of his leather seats being permanently damaged was his principle concern. "Has her water broke yet?"

"No," Gabbie panted, and then matched Mandy's swearing record as the two became one profane voice. He saw her squeezing Mandy's hand until both their knuckles were white. "Oh God, Mandy, I can't do this. Not without Case there…and if this is false labor they're going to need to sedate me for the real thing."

Once in the red ramp they made their way to the elevator, only to run into Ariel and Kevin.

"Honey," she cooed at the two girls. "Oh, my goodness, is it time?"

"I think so," Gabbie said between pants as she kept her eyes locked on the numbers of the elevator and her hands resting on a pillar.

"Get her a wheelchair," Ariel ordered, looking for the corner where they were usually parked.

"I'm good."

Mandy glared at her father who stood back from all the women.

"Prenatal visit," she tried to control her snarl, but it came out anyway.

"Yes, I went to yours, too, just so you know…well, most of them."

"Kevin, you came," a blonde entered the small area as a little girl with a cast on her arm hopped into his arms.

"Daddy!" she squealed.

* * * *

"A blonde, a redhead and a brunette walk into a bar," Mandy's evil laugh came out and she hoped she could hold back her rage. "Come on, Dad, finish the joke."

"Amanda, this is not the time," he warned, holding his hand out.

The elevator dinged and Ash tried to pull both Gabbie and Mandy into it, only to have them both stand firm. When another contraction hit, Gabbie gave into nature and followed him. Mandy looked over her shoulder at him.

"Take her up there, everyone's called."

"I'll protect her," he promised and the door closed.

"I'm sorry," the blonde said. "Kevin, what is going on here?"

Kevin stood with his daughter in his arms and petted her hair. The last time worlds collided like this a black hole was formed. Mandy assumed her father wished right now he could take a step back and enter one.

"Who are your friends, Kevin?" the woman asked again. Kevin just stood there staring blankly at them all.

"I'm Amanda, his daughter, not his oldest, but one of…gosh, I don't even know now. How many kids do you have with him?"

"I'm so sorry," the woman replied with solemn eyes. "I'm Molly. It was your mother that died of cancer so long ago."

"No, mine's the pregnant one who thought she was the other woman." Mandy pointed to Ariel who for the first time didn't have a glow about her. "Grace is the one who's very much alive after completing her chemo last summer."

"Last summer?" Molly turned to Kevin.

"We don't want Sandy to be late for her appointment," he said, heading toward the elevators.

"Brandon is ten."

"Oh, my God," Mandy squealed. "I have *another* brother."

"Another?" Molly shrieked. "Just how many kids do you have? How many women? Am I the only one stupid enough to think you'd marry me?"

"No," Ariel finally spoke, her words choked with tears. "Not by a long shot."

"Kevin, I want an explanation," Molly demanded.

"Not in front of Sandy."

"Why not, it seems I'm in the middle of a big old family reunion." Molly stood with her arms crossed as Kevin still seemed to be looking for an out. "You said your daughter was in high school and we couldn't be together until she graduated. She seems much older than that."

"Oh, Jillian's in high school," Mandy replied.

"So you have a little sister too."

"A few it seems," Mandy made a silly face to Sandy. "She's a cutie but how did she not get your eyes. I thought we all had your eyes, Daddy."

"He's my daddy."

"Oh, so you can be with her kids, but not mine," Ariel snapped.

"You are so missing the issue here, Mom," Mandy groaned. "How about the man you've been with for a quarter of a century has another family? And not the one you knew about."

"We're getting married, Kevin," Ariel said as she pointed at him. "That's final."

"Daddy and Mommy are getting married this summer," the little girl said. "I get to be the flower girl."

The little girl's words finally smacked Ariel enough to step back and grip Mandy's arm for support. Had her mother seen the light? Mandy looked into the dark caramel eyes and saw pain. Not emotional—this was physical.

"Something's wrong," she gasped, and Mandy frantically pressed the up button until the elevator came. The whole group stepped on and Ariel clawed Kevin's arm. He passed Sandy back to her mom.

"No, Daddy, I wanna stay with you."

"Just a moment, baby, my friend has an owie."

"I have an owie too," she cried, holding up her broken arm.

"Sandy," Molly warned, settling her daughter. "You know Daddy has responsibilities in other places."

"I don't care. I want my daddy." Stamping her feet, she broke down into a full blown temper tantrum and when the elevator dinged again Mandy stepped off with her mom and dad, leaving the latest woman alone with her child.

"I guess it was better not knowing about you," Mandy told her dad as they approached the labor and delivery desk. He didn't say anything.

"Can I help you?" A pleasant clerk with storks on her scrubs asked.

"This is Ariel Butler," Mandy began.

"We were coming for an ultrasound, but she started having stabbing pains," Kevin stated. "She's only five and a half months along. Please help her."

Mandy watched as he held Ariel close to him and took the brunt of her pain. Her knuckles turned white as she grasped his hand.

"Kevin, I can't lose another one," she sobbed.

"Another one?" Mandy asked. Her father just waved his hand in front of her face again.

A nurse had come around with a wheelchair and brought them back to a room.

"Who's all here with you today, Ariel?" the nurse asked as she helped her into the bed and started hooking her up to monitors.

"My daughter and…"

"Her fiancé," Kevin piped in.

"That's nice, finding love after so long."

"Is there still a heartbeat?" her mother frantically asked.

"One more sticker…" the nurse said and suddenly a fast thumping could be heard in the room.

Her mother strained to look at a brown box that had a number one-forty-three on it. A strip of paper came off the top and she sighed.

"I heard you say you can't lose another one. Ms. Butler, how many times have you been pregnant?" the nurse asked as she held the clipboard up.

"Seven, one live birth and this one."

"Seven," Mandy balked. "How did I miss the other five?"

Her mother showed a strength Mandy didn't know she had as she shook her head.

"You just thought mommy was lonely and that's why I cried so much."

Confusion ate at Mandy as she tried to comprehend and empathize. Instead she stared blankly. Multiple pregnancies and still her father came home each night to Mary Beth's mother. How did he find time for Molly?

"I couldn't explain how I was pregnant when I didn't date."

The nurse looked at the makeshift family in the room, but didn't judge.

"I've seen it all, don't worry," she assured them. After taking some other vitals, she got a history from Mandy's mom. Her father didn't let go of her hand the whole time. Even using one hand to pull a chair over so he could sit beside her. "The doctor will be in shortly. I'm sure we'll have to check a few things, but the heartbeat is strong."

"I'll leave you guys alone," Mandy said. "I need to check on Gabbie."

"Gabbie?" the nurse asked.

"Yes, I was bringing Gabbie Thomas in when I ran into them."

"She's one of my other patients. I'll take you to her."

Ash had Gabbie laughing so hard her phone was bouncing on her belly.

"What did I miss?" Mandy asked.

"Forget us…what did we miss?" Gabbie asked.

"You're about to have a baby."

"That is still to be determined. And the doctor said it would be at least a few hours before they could say anything for certain."

"Did they give you drugs?"

"A little bit?" Gabbie confessed with a giggle. "Now who was at the elevator?"

Mandy relayed her story while sitting on Ashton's lap. He had one hand on her back and the other on her thigh. Both were rubbing circles. It seemed right as they all burst into laughter. Then Case called them from the airport and Gabbie started crying because he was crying.

"You two are pussies," Mandy teased with jealousy, stretched, and then saw the time. "I should check on my mom."

"You want me to come with?" Ash offered.

"No, I'm good."

"Right," he sighed.

"I can't leave Gabbie alone."

"Yeah," Ash nodded. "That makes sense."

"I mean Case...he won't be here for hours."

Gabbie's eyes pooled again with tears as her father, Maury, walked through the door.

"Where's the bastard who got my baby pregnant?" he teased, only to stop short when he noticed Ash, not Case, was sitting in the rocking chair. "Case still in Arizona?"

"He's at the airport in Arizona right now, Dad," Gabbie assured. "You're still on deck."

"Who's picking him up when he lands?" Maury asked, and Ash's neck almost snapped off as he turned sharply. "I suppose that'll be me too?"

"You know it won't be me," Mandy smiled. "Don't worry, Ash was an all conference catcher in high school. I'm sure he'll do fine."

Ash's face paled, and Gabbie choked on some ice chips.

"Um, I have a doctor for that," Gabbie assured. "Ash, you know Case. Could you pick him up?"

"I'd love to help you out in any way you need," Ash said, and then cut his eyes at Mandy.

"Isn't he a peach?" Mandy teased as she wrinkled her nose.

* * * *

"Hey Mandy," Ash called to her in the hallway. "I know your family situation is really messed up right now, but I heard in most relationships the girl still introduces the guy to her family."

"But you already introduced me to your dad," she teased and lightly placed a kiss on his lips. "The guy doesn't until he's ready to get married."

"Funny."

"Ash, I just found out I have another brother and sister. And although the divorce has been finalized with Grace something tells me the Wallace kids aren't going to take kindly to more kids. I also learned my mother has been trying to have kids for the past two decades to outshine Grace's Madonna status."

Ash bowed his head. There were many parts of their relationship he didn't agree with, but he couldn't imagine not talking to Mandy every day. She'd proven over and over she actually was in this relationship and not playing around, but still he couldn't help wanting more. She'd become his everything and he still felt like an afterthought.

"Mandy," Maury called as he poked his head out of the room. "I think it's time."

"She said it would be hours."

"She's progressing a bit faster," the nurse said as she brought a baby warmer into the room.

"Where's Case?" Gabbie cried. "I can't have the baby without him."

"You couldn't conceive without him," Mandy teased while stroking back her hair. "Ash is ready to take off twenty minutes before his plane lands."

"But when does it land?" Gabbie whined and squeezed her father's hand.

"That's why I had one kid," he groaned. "Mama Mia, it's all coming back to me now."

"Because you were a good father who was there for my mom. Oh, my God, my baby won't love his daddy."

"I liked you better when you were sane," Mandy said.

"I liked you better when you slept around."

"You had your chance to be my boo-boo, instead you chose the breeder and look where we are now."

"Thanks for turning her down by the way," Ash said from across the room.

"Why are you still here?"

"Because we have an hour before he lands." Ash checked his phone and then shoved it back in his pocket. "Did she lose her mind in the last five minutes?"

"I'm fine," Gabbie said as tears drained down her cheeks. "I'm just scared."

"Hey, I got you girl," Mandy said. "I even have a guy to back me up. Crazy huh?"

"I told you they were worth having around."

"I have other ways I'm useful to her," Ash teased.

"She has been slightly manageable of late," Gabbie breathed out. The latest contraction must have passed.

Ash had never been present for the birth of a child. His place had always been in the waiting room with Karen, but now his place was here. Not because he'd gotten the girl pregnant, but because in Mandy's life Gabbie has always been there for her. She was her family, and Ash realized that he was becoming family now.

With each mention of stations and centimeters his knees got a bit weaker. Standing as close to the door as he could and still stay in Mandy's sightline, Ash reached for the door jamb. He hoped he wouldn't lose any of his manliness. At least, not into the waste basket.

"Gabbie," the doctor said while placing her hands on Gabbie's knees. "You're going to have to push pretty soon."

Ash looked at the clock on the wall. He was sure for Gabbie time was flying by, but for him the seconds ticked by like minutes. Mandy went to refill Gabbie's ice chips and gave him a quizzical look.

"You okay?"

"No...I mean, I know babies, but I tend to be there before and after, not during the whole..." His hands made a pushing motion and Mandy held in a giggle.

"Go pick up, Case, you'll probably have to do the whole loop a few times, but at least you won't be here."

"Thanks," he kissed her forehead and took off.

Chapter Twelve

"You don't have to give birth to someone to have a family."
—Sandra Bullock

"Where's Case," Gabbie screamed through a contraction while crushing Mandy's hand. "That son of a bitch better get his ass here."

"So I assume childbirth null and voids the swear jar," Case said as he entered the room with a swagger of confidence he shouldn't have been showing.

"I'm sorry," Gabbie snipped. "Did I interrupt your golf game to squeeze your big headed son out of my vagina?"

Case took her face in his hands and kissed her forehead.

"Only one of us can be in panic mode. You won the coin toss this time. I'll flip out later." Case took Mandy's place and she went to the door.

"Where's Ash?"

"Is your mom here?" Case asked. "I swear that's the room he went to."

"Oh, so he's just room hopping is he," Mandy growled.

"Hi," Gabbie cried. "Not your day. Get over here before I hurt you."

"You only have two hands."

Gabbie looked at them being held by her dad and husband, and then back to Mandy.

"You leave and I'll kill you."

"Over a guy? Please, I've got you, girl."

"Good," the doctor said as she poked her head over the drape above

Gabbie's knees. "It's time."

"No, I'm not ready," Gabbie confessed. "I can't be a mom."

"Yo, Vaulst," Mandy snapped, using Gabbie's maiden name. "You've been a mom for almost two years now."

"But I didn't do the hard part."

"You're raising them, honey, trust me, you're doing the hard part," Mandy said as she stroked Gabbie's bent knee.

"Are you sure this isn't false labor?" Gabbie asked the doctor. "I really can't feel much."

"Well, either I can see the head or you are in desperate need of a wax there."

"Nope, that's the head," Mandy said as she peeked between Gabbie's legs and marveled at the vision.

"Do you mind?" Gabbie asked right as Case pushed Mandy back to see. A tear escaped his eye.

"Who wanted me in the room?"

"Well, swap places with Dad."

"Um, no," Maury stated plainly. "Not unless you want them dealing with me and not them."

"Fine," Gabbie scowled. "But come up here, please."

Mandy came up to the top of the bed and helped lift Gabbie so she could bear down. The room filled with grunts and screams. She and Case had a connection that amazed Mandy. Their eyes would lock with every contraction as she pushed hard. Together they brought their son, Christian, into the world. Case had been tasked with following the baby if he left the room.

"Him first, every time," Gabbie reminded Case when he wanted to stay and make sure she was settled.

"Hey, slut, you just had a baby," Mandy teased as she helped get Gabbie settled and comfortable.

"Thank you for being here."

"You couldn't have kicked me out."

"Bullshit, I saw you want to leave."

"Only because I wanted my hearing when I go back to work."

"You wanna go tell everyone he's finally here."

"You have another son." Mandy hugged her friend tightly. "That's so damn trippy."

"I love you, you know that, right?"

"Never questioned it."

"Why don't you go check on Ash?"

"Oh, I'm sure he's left. It's been hours."

"I doubt it."

If for no other reason than to prove Gabbie wrong, Mandy left and went to the waiting room. Ash had his laptop out and was talking on the phone to someone.

"He can't attend that conference…okay, well is it more important to attend it for his cousin or get elected next year?" He saw Mandy and waved her over. "Look, you asked me to be an advisor. I'll be in town a few days from now. Ask him to table his reply until I can break down everything in person…great, see you later."

Setting the phone down, he closed his laptop and smiled at Mandy.

"So, do we have a baby?"

"Yep, a bouncing baby boy weighing more than a turkey."

"I doubt that, he was early."

"Okay, so he was still over seven pounds."

"Wow, impressive." Ash wrapped his arms around her and a chill shot through her body. After seeing Case and Gabbie, she suddenly felt like she and Ash were moving in that direction.

"Is my mom still here?"

"She was moved to the maternity ward so she could be monitored," he said. "Your dad is still with her."

"How about you come see the baby, and then I'll check in with my mom."

* * * *

Ash packed up his bag and wrapped his arm around Mandy's waist. He'd been the point man for Sarah and Mary Beth as they kept the twins occupied. Shooting a quick text, he knew soon the two girls would be on the way with the makeshift family the women created. Some out of necessity, like Mandy and Mary Beth who'd been pushed to the side by the family that should have loved them unconditionally.

That was when it hit him. Unconditional.

Mandy knew unconditional love, but not in the way he did. She understood it from friends who'd kill for each other, but not from family. Or lovers.

They knocked before entering the room where Gabbie was holding a beautiful baby boy with jet black hair. Having moved rooms, she was now in a double bed so Case could sit next to her. Fresh from a bath, Christian Thomas was swaddled in a blanket with his hand wrapped around his mother's finger. With little bow lips, he was taking in his exhausted mother as he focused on just her.

"Congrats you two," Ashton said. Case looked up from where he'd been staring at his son. "I texted the girls."

"I already called and asked Mary Beth to bring the kids," Gabbie said. "But thank you. You ready, Auntie Mand?"

"Beyond ready," Mandy said as she reached for the little boy and then sat in the rocker.

Mandy with children was a sight he'd never get enough of. Whether it was with a student, this newborn, or a stranger on the street, she became someone else. Or maybe she was actually being herself. She cooed and brought her nose to his head. Her eyes were sparkling as she promised him she'd be there to take him to his first strip club and make sure to slip him booze in high school.

Gabbie interrupted, "You can't babysit anymore."

"Did you hear that, Chris?" she cooed while nuzzling her nose against his. "I get out of changing diapers. Your Auntie Mand is a genius."

The baby yawned and snuggled against her chest as he slowly closed his eyes and fell asleep.

"You sure you don't want me to babysit?" Mandy asked with a smirk. "I've got that touch."

"Yeah, you do," Gabbie admitted with a soft smile.

Ash rested his hip on a counter at the edge of the room as he envisioned Mandy holding his kid. He could see the blonde hair and fair skin. Pink bow lips and long fingers holding tightly to her finger. The vision made him shift, and he was glad for the bustle that was the dynamic duo of Charlie and Claire.

"Mommy," they cried in unison as they rushed to the bed. Case stopped them from jumping on her.

"Where's my baby?" Claire asked, but Charlie had beaten her as he stood by Mandy.

"Can I hold him?" he asked softly.

"I'm going to give him back to Mommy, and then I bet you two can find a way to sit with him."

Mary Beth came in and gave hugs all around. When she entered the room Mandy's face paled and Ashton suddenly got a gut ache. Mixed in all the happiness was the discovery of more family. Mandy's head turned down and she went from open and loving to distant and closed off. Standing up she crossed to him and tapped him on his abs.

"I've got to go check on my mom." She looked at the family all snuggled together in the bed. "Bye-bye Thomas family."

"What's wrong with your mom?" Mary Beth asked.

"She's a few doors down. Something with the baby."

"I'll come with you."

"No...it's..." Mandy turned to Ash as if he were supposed to save her from this situation.

"Don't you want to visit with your friend?" he offered as an alternative.

"My brother or sister could be in danger, Christian is safe and needs family bonding time."

"Sister," Ash said. "Your dad told me when they moved your mom to a room."

"See," Mary Beth said. "We have to look out for our little sister. Your rule."

Mandy shivered, and then looked at the floor.

"It's been a long day, maybe I'll just check in with her in the morning," Mandy said. "I'm sure she's asleep."

"When was the last time you looked at a clock?"

"Why?"

"It's nine in the morning."

"Oh, well...I'm exhausted. I should go home."

"What did I miss?" Mary Beth asked, not letting Mandy back out of the conversation. He was glad her friends were there when she backed herself into a corner because he hadn't figured out how to do that. If he pushed too much, Mandy ran from him. He wanted to believe her coming back meant something, but in truth, he feared the coming moment when he pushed her too hard. That moment where he'd either break through to her, or lose her forever was quickly approaching.

The three of them stepped out of the room and Mandy looked like she was ready to hurl. Ash rubbed circles on her back as he tried to settle her nerves. Unlike Karen, she wouldn't melt and fall into him—Mandy pulled away. He wanted so badly to be her support, but she wouldn't let him. To her, he was a stranger unworthy of her trust.

"I'm walking a line here," Mandy finally confessed. "At some point I don't want to be the person around the hurt in your life. Even with my friends I've been the epicenter of every fucked up thing that ever happened to them. Ash...the only thing I could possibly bring to you is pain."

"This has nothing to do with you," Ash said. "This is your father."

"But I'm the messenger."

Mary Beth fell against the wall and slid down to the floor.

"Tell me," she ordered. "Whatever it is...I can...is it worse than Jillian?"

"Law enforcement isn't involved although I wonder why." Mandy sat on the floor next to her sister. "Our sister Sandy got her cast off today."

"Sandy?"

"She's probably four or five, her brother's ten. I couldn't sit around and hear his excuses to get the full story."

Mary Beth's face lost all its coloring as her arms tightened around her stomach.

"There's *another* woman?" she croaked out as if the words couldn't even travel from her brain to her lips.

"Yep, how good is his real estate business? My mom finally confessed she got money from Dad all the time to help me. Molly...that's the new woman..." Mandy twisted her fingers into a knot, then stretched. "She...well, it seemed like he spent a lot of time with the kids. The little girl knew him as her father."

Ash wanted to make himself scarce, but there wasn't anywhere he could really go. The intimate family issues were hard on Mandy. Hurt mixed with indifference as she tried to process the whole situation. None of it made sense to him. He wished he could understand the situation, but it was worse than any reality TV show. Her father's motivation confounded him. Sure, when he was younger Ash was all about quantity, but Mandy had really changed his perception of the quality of a woman. Having a family and children he knew would be the end of his wild ways. Actually, meeting Mandy had been the end of it. She matched his sexual need and even stimulated him on levels other than physical. Playing the fool, but constantly being able to respond to any topic.

"Is that how your mom ended up here?"

"Pretty much. She started having pains and they're observing her still. She lost five kids over the years. I guess your mom wasn't the only one who kept getting pregnant."

Karen and Sarah halted the discussion with their arrival. With a kiss to his cheek Karen awkwardly said hello. For the first time in a long while, perhaps ever, Ash was completely speechless.

It had been two months since Karen officially won the congressional seat, but Ash would never forget the conversation they'd had right after, no matter how much time passed.

"Ash, I won," Karen exclaimed when she got the news. The phone caught him between meetings.

"Congrats, Kare Bear, I knew you'd pull it off."

"Yeah, especially after they found those three boxes of votes just sitting in some guy's trunk." Her voice was filled with joy and nerves. "So, the freshman congresspersons are supposed to check in for orientation in two days."

"Is the party covering your last minute flight?"

"No, but Ash I need you to help me set up my office. Then we can start going over the bills set for the January session."

"I'm already in DC," he stated plainly. Not that he wasn't happy for her, but she'd barely checked on him except through Sarah.

"Perfect. I'll be flying in tomorrow morning. You can pick me up at Reagan at ten-thirty."

"Karen, I'm in DC because I have a job already. Not because I've been crossing my fingers on your win."

"What are you saying, Ash?" she asked as her words scratched at her throat. "You're abandoning me again? You know Howard doesn't do DC. He's moving on to a new candidate to back. I'll be all alone. You want me to be all alone?"

"You never needed anyone before." Ash sighed. "Karen...I was a crutch, you've done pretty damn well without me."

"You're my best friend, Ash. I haven't made a move without you in my whole life."

"How's Sarah?" he asked, hoping to change the subject or at least make her realize she wasn't the scared little girl who needed a hero standing behind her.

"Ash..." er voice caught again. "Can we at least have dinner tomorrow night?"

"Hell yeah, I'll use my RNC credit card." Ash waved down the hall to his next meeting. "And, Kare..."

"Yeah."

"I'm damn proud of you. For more than the win. I still expect to be your man of honor when you get married."

"I told you two not to look between Gabbie's legs," Sarah said as she approached the two women on the floor. "The vision cannot be unseen."

"That better not be advice from personal experience," Karen warned with a half smile.

"Sarah," he said. "Why don't you go meet the baby and let Karen and I have a minute."

The dinner two months ago had been strained, and the few times they'd passed each other he felt an arctic chill cut through him. A little of that ominous cold wafted over to him as they walked down the hall together.

After returning to the waiting room Ash wanted to sit, but Karen stood with her arms crossed, so he remained standing. His best friend for decades had a huge chip that needed to be knocked off her shoulder. He was exhausted and irritated enough to send it flying.

"So," she prodded without looking at him. "Talk."

"I think you should leave Sarah."

"What the hell, Ash. This conversation is bullshit and I'm not having it."

"I don't think you're good enough for her," he said as he caught her arm before she got away. "Sarah will kill for those three women and she'll support anything they do. Anything."

"They never abandoned her."

"Yes, they have," he yelped and then calmed himself. "They each have. Friends do that. Mandy is a great example. She's been dumped at one time or another by each of them. But they are always there to support each other on the big things."

"I'm in fucking congress. The first lesbian Republican to be there. Kind of a big thing."

He wished she'd quit defining herself that way, but she couldn't. Everyone was using that moniker. In his job, he'd get her to stop, but she wasn't who the party was worried about. At least not this week.

"And I'm not helping you get allies."

"What is it you do exactly?" she snarled. "We're in the same town, working for the same party, and I never see you."

"I'm not there that often. I get sent out, but I'm a fixer."

"Fixer. Like how you fixed my campaign."

"Your campaign didn't need fixing until you came out of the closet. People loved you. Hell, you didn't even need me on your arm. You could have stayed single. They still would have voted for you, but you dragged me along because you needed someone to cry to."

He placed his hands on her upper arms and rubbed up and down to calm not only her but himself.

"Also, to share the triumphs. Kare Bear, you never needed me around. I was your buddy. You taught me so much about politics and the game. You and Howard. Let me use the skills I've acquired. You don't need them and if I see you slipping up I'll step in, but you're the master."

"Stroking my ego..." She turned her head to the side, and he saw a tear roll down her cheek. He pulled her into a tight hug. "Sarah's not in DC with me. When I'm out there I feel alone."

"When I'm out there I'll stop by your office, but you have to promise to not be a bitch when I'm there."

"Oh please, I can't promise that to anyone."

"True. I guess I'll have to deal with it like always."

"You spoiled me." She snuffed into his shoulder. "It's all your fault."

"I know, but I passed the reigns to Sarah and she loves to spoil you. I had to be paid."

"Asshole." Karen pulled back, and she was that woman freezing on the dock again. She was his Kare Bear. His best friend since they were little. He'd loved her once, but it was so long ago he'd forgotten the emotion. Now she was the sister he never had. Much like with Mandy with her new family, he'd go to any extreme to protect her, but would also push her to walk on her own. "I better go look at that baby."

"Your uterus will scream when you see how cute he is."

"Shit, I better marry Sarah soon so we can have a few."

"Please. Even I can't fix an unwed, lesbian, cohabitating mother."

"I'm telling the party, that one is so easy." She pushed on his shoulder and bit her bottom lip. "I love you, Ash."

"I know, but only because I loved you first."

* * * *

Mary Beth's head rested on Mandy's shoulder. Guess the I'm-the-big-sister-deal was gone. Not that Mandy minded. She had Ash to lean on…wait a second. Mary Beth had Eli, her fiancé, as of a few months ago.

"I'm a whole ball of messed up," Mary Beth said through a crackled voice.

"Since when?" Mandy asked.

"I was just getting settled into my family again, and now…my mom doesn't want to help plan my wedding…my brothers are refusing to come home. Jillian has community service hours until she graduates I think."

"Too bad she won't be able to count them on her college application."

"College, don't get me started there. I missed the last week."

"I think you'll still pass."

"That's not the point."

"Then what is your rant about now?"

"Why are Dad's actions destroying all of our lives?" Tears rested at the edge of Mary Beth's eyes, begging to be released.

"Because I'm selfish," Kevin Wallace said as he approached them in the hall. "But it shouldn't, not if I'm a real father."

"Is there a reason you didn't relocate to Utah years ago?" Mandy snapped.

"I'll accept the comment." Kevin slid down the wall across from his two oldest daughters. "I fall in love."

"Or in bed," Mandy snarled. "You know, even though I love me, and I'm glad I'm alive, they have these great things called condoms. They've been around for decades."

"I'm Catholic."

"Do you really want to use that excuse with us?" Mary Beth asked. "Because the whole contraception thing is down on the list of naughty, bad things that send you to Hell?"

Kevin dropped his head and pulled his knees up to his chest.

"How many are there?" Mandy asked. "The hardest part of all of this for us is not knowing if we're going to run into a sibling at any moment."

"There isn't any more. I learned my lesson with your mom, Mandy, and didn't want a repeat with Sandy and Brandon."

"Can you clue me in on one thing?" Mandy asked. "How?"

"Women tend to not want to see the full picture. Not if you keep them happy."

"And you just destroyed two stable relationships," Mary Beth scolded as she spun her engagement ring.

"You're a different generation."

"But the same gender," Mandy said. "Thanks for that, though. Could be why I don't do relationships."

"What about the guy with you here now?" her father asked. "Your mom says he's with you."

Pulling in on her lips she shifted and tried to settle herself on that thought.

"You've been with quite a few. Could you choose just one?"

"I'm a man."

"That's up for debate," Mary Beth said. "And you might have just broken up the best thing that ever happened to Mandy with that statement."

Mary Beth got up and reached her hand out to Mandy. With a yank, Mandy was pulled to her feet, causing a head rush.

"Don't listen to him," she said. "All men aren't like that. Look at Case and Eli. Ash loves you."

"I'm just having fun. He's going to be moving away and he'll just have been a longer stop than the rest."

It was at that moment she saw Ash at the end of the hallway. She couldn't read him in that moment. He'd never been one to put on his politician face when it came to her. But if he hadn't nodded and turned toward the elevators she would have never known if he'd heard her. With that one look she saw the pain she caused underneath the diplomatic face of acceptance.

"Shit." Mandy didn't know what to do. Part of her wanted to run after him. Tell him she didn't mean it, but then there was part of her that liked a clean break with no recovery. Sadly, her sister was in love and demanded she be too. Shoving her toward the elevators, she demanded that Mandy apologize.

She didn't catch up to Ash until he was at his car. They stood on either side separated by the width of the vehicle.

"You were my ride," she said, stupidly. It was a lame excuse for why she was chasing him.

"I'm exhausted. My condo's only a few blocks from here. Can't you find a ride?"

"No." She crossed her arms. "No one will take me home."

"I'm sure you'll find another guy to take you. Or were you waiting for me to permanently move to DC first?"

"I figured I'd fuck you until then."

"Don't do me any favors."

Sarcasm was her first language. She wasn't sure how to speak…relationship. There were a lot of apologies and feelings involved. Two things she avoided like the plague. Her body on the other hand overrode her brain. Frickin' hormones…or was it her brain? When Ash opened his car door she ran over and stepped in front of him.

"I'm stupid. I fuck up. On a daily basis. You've put up with it all this time."

"That's because I stupidly thought you were being a grownup and trying to actually connect with me on a level that didn't involve lube and sex toys."

"Please, I never needed lube with you," she replied nervously. "Well except for...well, you were there."

"Yes, I was," he said and pushed her aside. "I thought you were too."

Ash started his car and left her standing in the parking garage watching his taillights trail away.

Chapter Thirteen

"Love is like a virus. It can happen to anybody at any time."
—Maya Angelou

The last thing Ash wanted to do was get on a plane back to DC. He wanted to see if Mandy could actually apologize, but what he really needed was sleep. Putting up with Mandy's hot and cold routine would be easier if he hadn't been up for over twenty-four hours. Crashing on his bed, he immediately passed out.

It was dark when he woke again. Messages filled his voicemail and email. It took him hours and a bottle of Advil to sort through it all. Munching on saltines, he came to the scary realization that he didn't even have the college special ramen noodles tucked away in his apartment. He didn't remember the last time he'd been to a grocery store for himself. Or when he'd spent more than a few hours in his own apartment. What more did Mandy need to understand he was with her?

Falling in love with her was the easy part. Smart mouth, great ass, and a heart three sizes too big. Although she only acknowledged two of these qualities. There was a time when stepping away was easy. But half of his headache came from the pain in his chest when he saw her in his rearview mirror standing alone in the parking garage. The last time he'd seen her that hurt he'd been there for her to yell at. He taught her about feelings. The ones she wanted to hide from. Then he'd left her alone.

Grabbing his keys from the counter, he stopped by their favorite Chinese restaurant. The smell filled his car, and he couldn't help eating egg rolls as he drove to her place to silence his rumbling stomach. With a knock, he held the take out bag in front of her peephole.

"Drew," she said as she opened the door. "Oh."

"Drew?" he asked and prayed Drew was a female, but the way Mandy said the name he doubted it. "Who's Drew?"

"A friend. I thought the take out was a bribe."

"It was. What is Drew bribing you for?"

"Come in," she said.

"Why won't you tell me?"

"Are you coming in or not?" she asked with attitude right as a man carrying a pizza showed up.

"Hi," he said. "I thought I was bringing the food, why'd you order Chinese?"

"Do I look like a delivery guy," Ash growled.

"Did I get the day wrong?" The man Ash assumed was Drew asked.

"This was preplanned? Like prior to today?" Ash asked as his head spun and his headache returned.

"I'm sorry, man, I can come by another time. It's not a big deal."

"Spending time with Mandy isn't a big deal to you?" Ash asked. "Is that because it happens all the time?"

"Did I miss something, Mandy?" Drew asked. "Have the rules changed?"

"Rules? There are rules?"

"Ash," Mandy said. "I think you should go."

"Right, I guess I overstepped my welcome." No longer hungry, he passed her the bag of food and left.

The flight the next morning kept Ash distracted as he used the in-flight Wi-Fi to keep up with his work. Actually, he never seemed to get a break lately. Troy was throwing more and more work at him. It was great for his bank account, but he thought it was more to pull him out to DC permanently. Between the cost of living and not being able to see Mandy every day, he wasn't exactly jumping at the opportunity. Then again, Mandy made it clear she'd made other plans.

He just wished he knew why. He'd floated the idea of her coming to DC with him last week. Maybe that was the problem.

Sitting on her couch, Ash had his laptop open and his feet resting on her ottoman. Mandy's toes were under his butt as she stretched out on the couch. The blanket was in the chair and she apparently didn't feel like snagging it and throwing it over her. Instead his ass was keeping her feet warm, so she was happy. Flipping through an application, she was making notes when she suddenly put them down.

"I have a headache, will you fuck me and make it go away?" she asked in such a fashion he looked at her unsure if the request was real.

"Can I finish my email?"

"I guess." She sighed and laid her arm across her forehead. "You want me to go in the bedroom and strip down or is here okay?"

Her straightforward manner had been a refreshing change in his life, even when it was at inappropriate times, like in public.

"Here's fine." He continued typing and her right foot moved from under him to his lap as she began stroking his cock to get him hard. "If your job is so stressful why not move to DC with me?"

"You're moving to DC?" she asked and retracted her foot.

"I'm thinking about it. Troy keeps sending more and keeping me there longer."

"That makes sense," she said, putting her foot back under his butt, and picked up another application.

"Hey, nothing is set in stone, but you're a teacher. You can do that anywhere."

"I'm a Montessori instructor."

"You think they don't have Montessori schools in Washington?"

"I'm sure they do, but do you not understand what we did?"

"What did you do?"

"We bought a daycare center, got it accredited with AMI, and opened a school. I have over five hundred applications this year. We're going to go from two classrooms to a minimum of four, but probably six or even nine if we can get the teachers. That's seventy students to three or four hundred in a year. It doesn't hurt that the school district had budget cuts and Mary Beth has helped us get grants for tuition, but Ash, I helped build something big. I helped create a school. Jasmine will have her own class next year."

"And you too, right?"

"I already have my own class. I'd get a new assistant."

"I'm sorry I brought it up." He closed his laptop and ran his hand up her leg to her knee. Most girls would have told him to shove it at this point. Mandy spread her knees apart and let him crawl between.

Kissing her belly at first, he snaked his way under her shirt and undid her bra. Her fingers ran through his hair and her nails scratched along his scalp, sending a shiver down his spine. Taking her breast into his mouth, he suckled her perked nipple while undoing her pants and removing her panties. It was the return trip that helped her get rid of her headache. His tongue split the center of her with lovingly long strokes as her flavor danced on it. Fingers joined in to create a rhythm and she pressed her core against his mouth. He rotated his fingers and she met his rhythm.

Her first orgasm had her arching as he linked his arms around her thighs. Swooping down and teasing her anus before returning caused the desired effect of her begging for him. Hard and trapped by his pants, he removed them and searched for a condom. Since meeting Mandy he'd learned to keep at least two in his pocket if he expected to see her in any capacity. Even if he might run into her at the grocery store, there was a chance they'd be having sex at any moment.

Sheathed, he surrounded his cock with her warmth. The strokes inside her body had her holding tightly to him. Her lips were hungry with the remnants of her flavor still on his tongue. Never did any spot seem too small. Instead they seemed to relish the fact they were closer than in a bed. In a bed, they'd roll and add to the experience, but the tightness of the couch kept them closer as she locked on him and held on for life.

"I want to ride you," she purred, and he pulled out, and sat on the couch.

Lowering herself onto him, he groaned as she knelt astride him. His fingers dug into her ass cheeks as she rode up and down on him.

"Oh fuck," she said and threw her head back.

The glow from the TV outlined her body. Her round breasts were right at his face. His right hand glided between them and circled her neck to bring her back to him. Pulling her back to him, their lips crashed against each other right as his balls tightened and released into her. Her core began to throb against him as she called his name into his mouth.

"Excuse me," the flight attendant woke him from the memory when she touched his shoulder. His mouth was dry as he took in his surroundings. "You need to put your tray table up and put away your computer."

"Right, thanks," he said, then realized he was hard as a damn rock. Looking at his seat partner, he was glad to see they were fast asleep and leaning against the side of the plane.

Shifting around he dug for his coat to cover his lap after he got ready for the landing. Running his fingers through his hair he tried to keep Mandy from his thoughts, but she was all he wanted. Maybe he should consider moving. Distance would be a good thing. It may be the only way he could get past her, because it was obvious she wasn't ready for love. The fucked up part was he not only was ready for it, he was in love with her.

* * * *

"I'm assuming you didn't order Chinese," Drew asked as they sat down at the table after getting plates and forks.

"No, I didn't."

"Who's the guy?"

"His name is Ash and we…" Mandy didn't know what they were now. She didn't understand the whole fight and get back together thing. "I don't know what we are."

"All right," Drew said and pulled out the Chinese takeout cartons. "Do I have to eat this?"

"That would be for me." Mandy opened the chicken and peapods and dished it out onto her plate.

"I thought you only ate fried rice."

"Guess you don't know me very well," she said.

"How long have you known Ash?" Drew asked.

"About six months, why?"

"I've known you for ten years now, and I didn't know that," Drew said while snagging a piece of pizza.

"What's your point?" Mandy replied as she smelled the chicken and peapods, only to have her stomach clench…from guilt.

"Mandy, you shoved him away. I doubt it was because of me."

"Then why did I do it?" she asked and took a bite of her food.

"You pay your debts immediately," he said. "I've texted you a dozen times since I helped out Jill. I don't ever remember you telling me no. I also don't remember you ever being with one guy."

"I'm sorry, is there a point to this story?"

"Okay, let me ask you something. You have two ways to pay off the debt you owe me. The first is to spend the night with me and try to break our record of orgasms."

"That sounds like fun," Mandy said, but even she could feel the disconnect and the fact she didn't mean it.

"The second is you tell me about Ash and admit any feelings or thoughts you have about him."

"I vote for number one."

"You love him," he said. "Does he treat you well?"

"I voted for number one, fuck me into oblivion." Mandy set down her fork and stood.

"Sit."

"Do you want me to call you officer?" she asked as she arched her eyebrow.

"Mandy, you've been fucked up since I met you."

"I love you too, asshole."

"Something is different about you. I could tell when you asked for the favor. I just never imagined you actually found someone. Don't throw it away."

She hated that Drew actually cared about her in a strange way. They were never more than fuck buddies, but still there was a part of him looking out for her. It wasn't a sisterly thing. He was a friend. When he'd been dating someone he still looked out for her. Even arresting a guy who'd pissed her off.

"I like Ash, but I don't fall in love. You know that."

"Invite me to the wedding," he said as he stood up and kissed her forehead.

"There's no wedding."

"Go get him back."

"No."

"Mandy, do you want your sister to go to jail?"

"Are you fucking kidding me?" Mandy screeched.

"Yes, it's too late. She already had a deal in place." Drew picked up his pizza box. "Let yourself be loved. Please, for me."

He gave her a hug and left.

"Are you fucking kidding me?" Mandy called out and then flopped on the couch.

Flipping on the TV she searched for the worst reality TV show she could find. Anything to take her away as she ate the damn chicken and peapods, fucking Ash knew her. *Damn it.*

The last thing she was going to do was grovel for him. He was leaving, he'd be moving soon. Sure, he offered to take her along, but how could she be with someone who didn't understand how important the Growing Strong Montessori was to her. Or her mafia sisters. Case's stupid nickname for the four of them. Even when Gabbie was in the middle of having a baby, she was still worried about Mandy. Mary Beth gave up holding Christian to make sure Mandy was okay. Her best friends would never leave her, and there was no way she'd ever leave them for a man. Not even one she'd fallen in love with.

The door opened and Sarah came in. The sun was shining through the window. Mandy wiped the drool from her cheek as she adjusted to the time.

"You know, throwing off your sleep schedule during spring break is only going to make it harder to get back on schedule."

"Mom...no, it's just my annoying sometime roommate."

"Hey, is Ash back in Washington?" she asked.

"Like I would know."

"Did you two have a fight?"

"What would make you say that?" Mandy asked, sat up and let the world swirl around her for a moment.

"Mary Beth."

"Frickin' gossip," Mandy grumbled as she rubbed the crook in her neck.

"I heard he had to go back to Washington," Sarah said as she plopped in the chair. "You didn't drop him off at the airport, I assume."

Mandy raised her eyebrow at Sarah who reached for the remote and turned off the TV.

"Why are you here?" Mandy asked.

"I pay rent."

"Right," Mandy said and waved her off.

"It's none of my business—"

"Then don't speak."

"You two are good together."

"Again, it's none of your business."

"Fine, but just once I'd like to see you put forth a little effort when it comes to a relationship."

"I totally threw myself into this."

"No...no, you didn't," Sarah said. "In fact, you seemed to be looking for outs at every turn. Ash was the one who kept the two of you together. One-sided relationships never work. But I know you don't ever like to put yourself out there."

"Hey, I put myself out there."

"No, you put yourself out. There's a difference. Take a chance. Ash will be there for you if you let him."

"Exactly how could I do that?"

"I don't know. I'm not the one who's been dating him for half a year. You have. What sacrifice could you make that would let him know you actually care about him?"

"Like I would know."

"You have three days till he comes home. Figure it out, or you're going to lose him forever. Can you live with that?"

* * * *

"I know," Ash said as he exited the plane with his Bluetooth in and Troy in his ear.

"I thought it was a simple question. You have no job, no girl, and no prospects in Minnesota. I'm offering you all of that."

"A girl. Yeah, I'm not fond of the ones that need to be paid by the hour."

"Actually there are a few women who are looking to be hooked up with an up and comer."

Great, another woman interested in how he can help her, not being with him. Recovering from Mandy hadn't been an overnight thing, it also showed him he could be part of something, not a piece of it. Still deep in the midst of the pain, he wasn't about to toss lemon juice on that open wound. Just the thought of her made his chest ache as if a vice had been turned flush. The idea of spending time with one more woman was as appealing as do it yourself open heart surgery, and only slightly less damaging.

"Last I knew, I wasn't a prince in line for a throne." The words scratched against his throat.

"I need to get you to reset your brain."

"My brain is fine," Ash said while grabbing a paper and tossing a few dollars on the counter. The girl working had come to know him and didn't take offense since he usually flirted more than he should. Maybe Mandy was right—neither of them were ready and he'd been lying to himself. "Look, I need to check in on my dad and make sure everything's in order, and then I'll get back to you."

"The window is closing."

"So you've lectured me for the last three days," Ash sighed while stepping on the escalator that took him past the secured zone and down to baggage claim. Rolling down, he saw the six panels of glass and a few people standing on the gray tile. "Troy, trust that I'm aware of all you are...offering."

"You okay there?"

"I have to go."

Ash hung up as he reached the bottom of the escalator, only to see a giant piece of poster board with purple and silver glitter spelling Magilla. Mylar balloons were strung from the top of the sign with *Missed You* and hearts exclaiming love. Behind the sign was Mandy with a bunch of carnations.

With a swish the doors slid open and he stepped to Mandy who had tear-filled eyes as she leaned against the wall.

"You forgot the box of chocolates."

"I got you a *Snickers* just in case you were being a bitch." She pulled it out of the center of the flowers. "You know, hunger and crap. At least that's what they say on TV."

"Are you fucking Drew?" It was rude, but it had been the question keeping him up at night and distracting him for the past few weeks.

"Presently? No. I'm standing here with a tacky sign and flowers."

"Did you fuck him the other night?"

"Nope." Mandy shifted uncomfortably. "I wanted to. I owed him a favor. Then you showed up, and I didn't want to be that person anymore."

"What favor did you owe him?" he asked, still not ready to let himself give in to her, love or no love.

"He's a cop in Oakdale, where Jillian stole the car from."

"And you got her sentence reduced in exchange for sex."

"No, I just used sex as a bargaining chip," she confessed.

"Did he pick up the chip?"

"I didn't throw it down. Instead I spent the night talking about you."

"How did that work out?"

"My debt is paid in full," she solemnly replied. "He was happy for me. You know, finding a guy and what not."

Ash couldn't believe the story she told. It was a bit too convenient.

"Didn't Jill get in trouble in November?"

"Yes."

"And between then and now…"

"Drew would check in, but I was unavailable."

"Because you were with me?"

"You're my boyfriend. Or were my boyfriend."

Ash studied Mandy. He wanted to be mad at her. He wanted to hate her more than air, but at the same time, he missed the feel of her body against his. The snarky comments that spewed from her mouth because she'd never been able to give herself to anyone. All of it had been missing, and worst of all, he wanted it in his life.

"Are you picking me up at the airport?" he asked as he looked around.

"If I were?"

"It would mean you loved me."

Mandy stared him down as her tongue seemed pressed against her back teeth. He saw the divide between them crumbling as each second passed. Locked in a look that made him hunger to taste her, he leaned in, only to be caught off guard when a paper landed between them.

Pulling back, he noticed Mandy was holding the paper.

"Wanna go back through security?" she asked.

"Why?" he stumbled, having been duped by her again. Living with her, he might as well be standing on an exercise ball. Even when he found the strength to balance, she'd just kick it to the side.

"Let's go to Vegas."

"Vegas? I just got home. I don't even know if I want to be around you and you ask me to go to Vegas?"

"You leaned in. You tried to kiss me," she said with childlike zeal as she stuffed his sign in a trashcan and skipped to the set of escalators that led back up to the ticketing area. "Come on, Magilla. You know you can't resist me."

"I most certainly can," he spat as he stood firmly until she turned around and walked backward so she could keep her eyes on him.

"Ash, you know I'm going to fuck up six ways from Sunday," she said as she waved the tickets in the air and he stood there like a dunce holding his flowers. "But you also know I love you, so get your hunk-tastic ass on the escalator or we'll be late for our flight."

"Did you say love?" he asked as he began to follow her.

"Gotta catch me to find out." Mandy hopped on the escalator and he had to run the stairs two at a time just to wrap his arms around her as they rolled to the top. "I love you, Magilla. Never thought I'd actually say that in my life, but I love you more than I hate air."

He smiled as he stroked her cheek with his thumb cradling her head in his hand. "'Bout time you figured it out."

His lips brushed against hers and he dropped the flowers. Crushing against her body he knew this wasn't a fluke. She wanted him. It wasn't a need. She'd taken the step, and he was going to make sure, no matter what, she'd never regret the decision because he'd always be there for her.

"Why Vegas?" he asked as they got closer to the TSA agent.

"Cheapest last minute flights I could find. Hope you don't mind flying coach."

"No." He smirked.

She looked at him with a puzzled look.

"So," he asked before he stepped through the x-ray, leaving Mandy to stare at him while a security guard held her back. "You think a senator could be elected if he married his wife in Vegas?"

Epilogue

"The greatest gift that you can give to others is the gift of unconditional love and acceptance." ~Brian Tracy

Mandy woke in a suite Liberace puked in. Floor to ceiling windows let her see past the strip to the mountains as the sun was cresting. The bed was round! Round! She shook her head and rolled in the silken sheets to find Ashton still asleep. Padding along the fur carpet, she wandered into the bathroom to take care of her needs, just to stub her toe on a glowing glass table. Surely, she should have seen that, but alas all she could do was let out a barrage of swear words as she fell back to the bed.

"My blushing bride," Ash grumbled as he wrapped his arm around her stomach and nipped her backside.

"Your klutzy bride, more likely. And who says I'm marrying you?"

"You did it before."

"Ten years ago. I was dumb and you were hot."

"Was hot?" Ash asked as his nips hit her ticklish spot by her ribs.

Running her fingers through his hair, she leaned down and their lips met. After a full night without their kids, she had to say a little more loving before their friends arrived for their recommitment ceremony did sound like a good idea. Something about that fifth month of pregnancy always shot her libido into overdrive. Then again, the fact Ash had become sexier with age didn't help it either.

"I can't believe you're making me marry you," he teased as he rubbed his hand over her belly. "All because I knocked you up."

"Gabbie's just pissed she didn't get to come the first time. I'd promised her she could fly to Vegas when we got married. Of course, I was sure I wouldn't be marrying you, so it was an empty promise."

"Speaking of which," Ash began right as the patented Gabbie knock meant Mandy would need to put on clothes. Wrapping herself in a robe, she was careful to avoid the table of hurt when she opened the door.

"It's early," she groaned then looked at the lineup in the hallway.

Her family, those related by blood and those related by bonds that were deeper, crowded in the hall. There were only three girls she was interested in, though.

"Mama," the girls called as they took off down the center of the crowd running from their aunties.

The oldest, Elizabeth, was already in her flowered dress for the ceremony. With rich, dark hair braided down to her waist, she was the first to wrap her arms around Mandy's waist. At seven, she'd been Ash's election surprise.

Lexi at three somehow beat her older sister, Ryder, the terror of Sarah's classroom. With the three of them locked on her, Mandy turned to see Ash smirking back at her. They'd come out a few days before the girls and, although they enjoyed their alone time, she was happiest cuddling with her girls and Ash at home.

"Daddy," the girls squealed again as they took off to attack Ash, and Mandy pulled herself back up.

"Did everyone have to come up here?" Mandy asked her friends and all their kids as they piled in to her hotel room. Sure, it was a suite and big enough for them all as half crashed on the large U shaped couch, but still five minutes ago, Ash and Mandy had been butt naked…Ash might only be wrapped in a sheet. With a quick glance the worry left as she saw the top of Ash's waistband.

Gabbie and Case had added another girl to their family, Cassandra, Lexi's best friend. The long and lanky teenaged Charlie stretching out while playing on his phone and Christian at his hip as usual. Claire, still a fashonista, was happily braiding Ashleigh's hair, Sarah and Karen's youngest. Their six year old, Howie was pressed up against the window with Mary Beth and Eli's middle child Antonio. Luke was holding the latest addition to the Growing Strong Mafia, Laura. At six months old,

Mary Beth hadn't wanted to bring her daughter, but they were sisters after all.

"Is it too late to elope again," Ash asked as he got out of bed with Lexi in his arms.

"Yes, Senator," Mandy said as she put her arm around his waist. "You owe your seat to the mafia, and they always collect on their debts."

THE END

About the Author

Michel Prince is an author who graduated with a bachelor degree in History and Political Science. Michel writes young adult and adult paranormal romance as well as contemporary romance.

With characters yelling "It's my turn, damn it!!!" She tries to explain to them that alas, she can only type a hundred and twenty words a minute and they will have wait their turn. She knows eventually they find their way out of her head and to her fingertips and she looks forward to sharing them with you.

When Michel can suppress the voices in her head she can be found at a scouting event or cheering for her son in a variety of sports. She would like to thank her family for always being in her corner, and especially her husband for supporting her every dream and never letting her give up.

Michel has been awarded Elite Status with Rebel Ink Press in 2013, the service award for her local RWA chapter Midwest Fiction Writers in 2013 and 2014, won Sweetest Romance at IREA and is a PAN member of RWA. She lives in the Twin Cities with her husband, son, and dog, Bolt.

You may contact the author at:

www.michelprincebooks.com
www.facebook.com/michelprincebooks
https://twitter.com/michelprince1

www.ingramcontent.com/pod-product-compliance
Lightning Source LLC
Chambersburg PA
CBHW052136170626
46812CB00004B/1460